Some Trick

Helen DeWitt

SOME TRICK

thirteen stories

A NEW DIRECTIONS BOOK

Published by arrangement with the author.

Grateful acknowledgment is made for permission to quote from the following:

"We're Off to See the Wizard" (from *The Wizard of Oz*)
Music by Harold Arlen, lyric by E. Y. Harburg. Copyright © 1938 (renewed) Metro-Goldwyn-Mayer Inc. Copyright © 1939 (renewed) EMI Feist Catalog Inc. Rights throughout the world controlled by EMI Feist Catalog Inc. (publishing) and Alfred Music Publishing Co., Inc. (print). All rights reserved. Used by permission of Alfred Publishing, LLC.

"Don't Think Twice, It's All Right"
Copyright © 1963 by Warner Bros. Inc.; renewed 1991 by Special Rider Music. All rights reserved. International copyright secured. Reprinted by permission.

"Let's Call the Whole Thing Off" (from *Shall We Dance*)
Music and lyrics by George Gershwin and Ira Gershwin. Copyright © 1936 (renewed) Ira Gershwin Music and George Gershwin Music. All rights on behalf of Ira Gershwin Music Administered by WB Music Corp. All rights reserved. Used by permission of Alfred Publishing, LLC. Reprinted by permission of Hal Leonard LLC.

A publisher's note begins on page 195.

Manufactured in the United States of America
New Directions Books are printed on acid-free paper
First published clothbound by New Directions in 2018

Library of Congress Cataloging-in-Publication Data
Names: Dewitt, Helen, 1957– author.
Title: Some trick : 13 stories / Helen DeWitt.
Description: First edition. | New York : New Directions Publishing, [2018]
Identifiers: LCCN 2017055363 (print) | LCCN 2017057388 (ebook) |
ISBN 9780811227834 | ISBN 9780811227827 (acid-free paper)
Classification: LCC PS3554.E92945 (ebook) | LCC PS3554.E92945 A6 2018 (print) |
DDC 813/.54—dc23
LC record available at https://lccn.loc.gov/2017055363

2 4 6 8 10 9 7 5 3 1

New Directions Books are published for James Laughlin
by New Directions Publishing Corporation
80 Eighth Avenue, New York 10011

Contents

Here Is Somewhere vii

Brutto 3
My Heart Belongs to Bertie 25
On the Town 43
Remember Me 65
Climbers 77
Improvisation Is the Heart of Music 103
Famous Last Words 115
The French Style of Mlle Matsumoto 131
Stolen Luck 141
In Which Nick Buys a Harley 157
Trevor 165
Plantinga 175
Entourage 183

PUBLISHER'S NOTE 195
AUTHOR'S NOTE 197

Here Is Somewhere

If ever if ever a wiz there was
The Wizard of Oz was one because
Because because because because because

'I have nothing to give you but that's all right because
Knowledge of lack is possession
Recognised absence is presence
Perceived emptiness plenitude.
To have not
And know it
Is to have.'

Some trick.

'True wisdom is knowing you don't know.'
The Scarecrow hadn't the brain to see through it.
He bought it.
'I don't understand,' he thought.
'That's my wisdom, that is.'

'What would you do with a heart but try not to hurt?'
The Tin Man hadn't the heart to disappoint him.
He thanked him.
'I feel nothing,' he thought.
'But I wouldn't hurt a Behaviourist.'

'Courage is not being fearless, it's facing your fear.'
The Lion hadn't the nerve to say he was scared.
He roared.
'I'm still terrified,' he thought.
'But you'll laugh if I say it.'

Next time someone tells you desire
Is a trick of grammar
Tell him
If what I have is what I said I wanted
It's not what I wanted
I know what I want
But I don't know its name.

Could you say that to a puzzled, hurt, frightened old wizard?
Of course not.
You'd say
'Thanks very much then.'

Some trick.

But Dorothy? I don't B E L I E V E Judy Garland could fake it.
I think she was glad Technicolor was only a dream
Glad to find she had never left home
Glad to wake up in grey black and white.

Because because because because because

Some Trick

Brutto

Her father was an engineer. He worshipped Daimler, so there was only one career for him. He had no particular opinion on the Jews; if you would ask him he would not be interested, probably it was an inadequate race but he wasn't interested. If you are an engineer the only thing you care about is machines. A human being is never going to be as perfect as a machine so it is not interesting to an engineer to think about racial purity.

She was saying things to Nuala so people looking at the paintings would not feel they were under surveillance. It's always a bit like working in Top Shop or Dorothy Perkins or Wallis, some shop where they have this etiquette of leaving the customer at arm's length.

These open days are hard at first, but you get used to them. People come into the studio and sometimes they walk straight out. Or they look at the paintings and they want to see something figurative lurking behind it all when there is no behind. But the paintings are so explosive they don't know what to do with it. And you're sitting there with this poxy table with a bowl of cheese doodles and you feel like a complete wally.

This bloke was walking about.

Sometimes this mania for hospitality takes possession of you. She asked if he would like a cheese doodle.

He said I'm fine thanks.

He had an Italian accent. He had one of these haircuts that all the men have these days, where there is hardly any hair, it is like short fur on the skull. His eyes were this light glowing grey, like those little monkeys, those lemurs that you see on TV or at the Zoo, and he had this pulpy, kissy mouth. He was standing by 1.1.4.

When people number paintings they do it the wrong way. You get an idea while you're working on a painting and you have to do it in another painting because otherwise you would use the first painting. It's like taking cuttings from a plant. So if you just use ordinal numbers you lose all that. You lose a distinction, because sometimes a painting is just out of the blue.

Sometimes you know there's a gap between one painting and another, that was a painting you didn't do, so you can show that with the number and that's good, the missing painting still has its number like a name on a grave.

He was wearing a black t-shirt and a black cashmere jacket and black jeans, these really expensive jeans, and these red cowboy boots.

The paint is always white, this fat gloopy stuff, and people have never seen anything like it. Sometimes it's 20 centimetres thick or maybe more, it can take a year before it's really dry. You have to give people really careful instructions when they buy one. Once this gay couple fell in love with this painting that was really not ready to be moved but they said they would obey her instructions *implicitly* and of course Serge was keen to make the sale so they took it and this great big *splodge* fell off on a brand new carpet.

You weren't supposed to live in the studio but of course people did surreptitiously.

If you are working with white you get fanatical about having the specific white, and you are in a constant state of panic that the white will be discontinued. Robert Ryman liked to work with a white from Winsor & Newton called Winsor White, so when Winsor & Newton decided to discontinue production he bought a whole consignment and filled a closet with it, and this is what you can afford to do if you are Robert Ryman. So this is one problem of being poor, that you can be cut off from the work you would go on to do by the discontinuance of a white. This is something people can understand, the expense of materials, these things you can touch and see. But if there is a painting that would be dry in a week and another painting that would be dry in six months there is that pressure to paint something that will survive in the time you know you can pay for. So that is the trade-off, the more white you buy the less time you can pay for. So you are always living hand to mouth.

She was two months behind on the rent on the studio. If she would get kicked out she would never find another studio for £300 a month.

Serge owed her £5,000 from the London Art Fair *two years* ago.

The bloke was looking at 1.1.11111.1.

Nuala was sitting on the tall stool to keep her from feeling like a complete prat.

She said people didn't talk about the War when she was growing up. There was this very tidy surface and you didn't know there was anything but the surface. They didn't talk about the camps. So then when she was 16 Max told her about them and she understood the Baader-Meinhof, she wanted to blow up a building. Her father made her do the Geselle which was three years of hell. She knew if she stayed she would kill herself. So she hitchhiked for about 6 years around Asia.

When you are that age you don't think about the cut-off age for the Turner Prize. You don't realise that the people who are going to get their work to a certain level before the cut-off are not hitchhiking around Asia. If you would realise it you would not be able to do anything about it, because if you would not hitchhike around Asia you would not be an artist. So you can't say if I would have gone to art college then.

Nuala had helped with the cheese doodles and twiglets and there was juice. Wine would be better but if it's crap wine what's the point? And what would it be but crap wine?

She said when she was growing up her father would not let her do the Abitur, he thought she was too thick, he made her go into an apprenticeship in dressmaking. They sat in this *cellar* and everything had to be done just right, making buttonholes, if you did it wrong you had to do it again and that was 3 years. At the end you had to do a Gesellenstück, it's quite an old-fashioned word, maybe they don't have it in English, to show you had mastered the craft. It had to have all these features, this special collar and these special cuffs and special pockets.

She still had the suit she made.

There was a wardrobe off a skip in a corner. She went to the wardrobe. It had a special padded hanger.

May I see?

The Italian guy was standing at her shoulder.

She said: Yeah, OK, why not.

It was a suit in a scratchy woollen cloth. It was a dirty mustard brown. You did not get to choose what you would make up, it was a chance for the dressmaker to get rid of fabric she could not use, other places treated the apprentices better, she had heard. The suit had buttoned epaulettes and cloth straps with a button at the cuffs and a cloth half belt, and pockets with buttoned flaps, and of course a lining, and self-covered buttons. It had piping in dark brown. It had three semi-pleats above each breast, each set interrupted by a pocket. It hung on its hanger, this baleful garment that no one would ever wear because of the hatefulness of the cloth and the cut and the straps and the stitching, and all this time the garment had been locked up in a wooden coffin with no one to look at its madness.

He said: Ma che brutto!

He said: Take it over to the light.

In the white light of the studio the sullen mustard wool, the psychotic stitching, the brutal dowdiness snarled at the world.

He said: Madonna!

He said: When was it made?

She said: 1962.

He said: Can you still do this?

She said: I don't do this any more.

He said: I want this.

She said: It's not for sale.

He said: I want 20 of these.

She said: I am not a dressmaker.

He said: No no no! Who would wear such a monstrosity? What do you take me for? No. You are an artist. I will give you £1,000 apiece.

She said: I might be able to do one more.

He said: That's not enough. I want to have a show. I need another 19.

He said he would have a show in his gallery in Milan.

He said: The paintings don't interest me.

He said: You'll get the normal terms, 50% split, the 20 grand is up front.

She said maybe she could find someone to help her and he said No. It's got to be you or the deal is off. You know you can't find someone to do this kind of work.

He said: Will you be able to find—

No, we go look for the stuff together.

Maybe we go to Leipzig, I think, they got a lot of ugly old stuff left from before 89, yeah I bet we can do it.

She did not know what to do because she just couldn't.

Then Serge came in, he had been down the hall in Danny's studio schmoozing with a buyer who maybe would take something for his company headquarters. Serge said: *Adalberto!!!!!!!!* Christ, I'd no idea you were in town.

So maybe you can imagine if five lizards would be in an icebox and somebody would put them up the back of your jumper so they would be crawling up your back with their cold claws, because realistically how many people in the artworld would there be with the name Adalberto—

Adalberto said: Yeah I'm really excited about this piece she did back in the 60s.

At first Serge got excited because of the sale and then he started to be pissy because Adalberto wanted to be the gallerist for the material in Italy so Serge would not get a commission, but Adalberto said No no no we're not gonna argue this is the most exciting work I've seen in a long time but I gotta have a free hand to take it where it needs to go, we'll work something out, we're not gonna be assholes about it.

It would never have arisen in the first place if Serge had paid her the £5,000 he owed her from the London Art Fair.

People were coming into the studio and looking at the paintings and all it would have taken was just one to buy just one.

She could tell that Serge was flattered and Adalberto was talking about dinner and she could tell he would bamboozle Serge into agreeing to anything.

Serge was thinking he could make some good contacts, and if he knew the right people he could get some publicity for his next opening, maybe Nick Serota would come, if Nick Serota would come it would be the bees knees.

She was completely skint.

She said she would have to think about it because she was not working in that tradition at all, and Adalberto said Yeah, sure, think about it, I have to go to New York next week so it would be good to go to Leipzig tomorrow so you can do some before I come back.

Adalberto said: Look, let's not pussyfoot around, I give you £2,500 apiece, that's 50 grand.

Serge was just standing there completely gobsmacked.

It's easy to say you can just walk away from it.

They flew first class to Leipzig out of City Airport. It was sort of the way you are always imagining it would be if you would get your lucky break, you know you are sleeping in a sleeping bag on a concrete floor and there is no heating and no loo but you think maybe one day you will be discovered, but meanwhile everybody is poor. If she would have lunch with Serge he would always go somewhere *really cheap*, and then they would go Dutch. And meantime Serge had given her the scoop on Adalberto, she had heard stories of course but it turned out he was this really hot potato, he was on the committee for the Venice Biennale so if Adalberto would like her work it would be phenomenal.

When they got to Leipzig they took a taxi to this posh hotel. Adalberto said he did not know if they would find what they were looking for in Leipzig, maybe they would have to go deeper, but they would maybe have some luck.

The thing that is famous in Leipzig is the passageways, these arcades. The most famous is the Mädler-Passage, but they have them all over, these passageways between streets that were built to be fashionable places to be seen, with shops selling things that fashionable people would want to buy, well you can imagine how popular that would be in a socialist republic. So they would go down an arcade and out into the street and down another arcade, looking for this thing Adalberto had in his head.

If you would go to East Germany in those days it was still the way it was under the Communists. You would go into a shop and it was like a time warp. A shop would have a little window display and it would be a pair of knickers and a packet of tights. You forget what people used to wear, so if you suddenly see it in a shop window you can't believe it. You can't believe that it went on looking completely normal. So they would be drawn into these shops that were not selling what they needed, because it was like a museum.

Adalberto was still wearing the red cowboy boots. He saw all this stuff and he went completely mad. He would see a garter belt in a glass case in a little shop and he would be like a man possessed, he would buy maybe the entire supply of garter belts. He would ask what is the German for this, and it would be a garter belt or an antique pair of knickers or a slip.

Then he would say: We gotta be focussed, we gotta be totally focussed on this, this is gonna be, what is that word, humongous. Estupendous.

Then they found a haberdashers.

It had these bolts of this disgusting beige jersey. Adalberto said: We gotta be focussed. We gotta be totally focussed.

He said: Ask where they keep the suiting materials.

So they went to the back and she thought she would throw up. There were these bolts of woollen cloth.

Adalberto was saying *Madonna*.

There were all these conservative colours that you don't see any more, this navy blue, navy blue is the hardest colour to match so it dates really obviously because the idea people have in their head of a dark neutral blue changes over the years, people in the fashion industry, the way they perceive a dark blue is affected by the other colours they are working with at the time. So there was this navy blue that had survived like a finch in the Galapagos, and a prehistoric brown, and some greys that also date really quickly. They were not utilitarian colours, just colours of cloth that was meant to end up in respectable clothes and you would not imagine the body inside and you would not imagine that people would sign a form to put people on a train to go off and be butchered.

Adalberto was saying: Ma che *brutto*! Che *brutto*!

He was saying: If we were not coming now it would be too late!

And he was saying: You are the one with this special training, you must pick what you would work with, what they taught you to work with.

She said: I can't.

He said: If I say something maybe it corrupts what you were taught.

She said: I can't.

He said: OK, OK. Look, we take everything back with us, I don't have time for this, when we get back you decide what you want to use.

He went to the saleswoman and he pointed to the back: Ich will alles verkaufen.

You could tell she was not used to customers who did not know German. You could tell Adalberto was not used to people who would not roll over and play dead if you would give them a lot of money.

She said: Kaufen, Adalberto. You are saying you want to sell everything.

In the fullness of time, said Adalberto. I will. But OK. Ich will alles kaufen, Madame.

But she couldn't stand it, all this money sloshing around when she kept *agonising* about £600 for the studio, and where she would put the paintings if she could not pay the rent.

So she said: No. It's stupid. There's nowhere in the studio to put it all.

She said: Look, Adalberto, go away. Go for a walk. Go to a café. I can't think with you standing there saying *che brutto*.

This was one of the luckiest things she ever did.

OK, said Adalberto. You're the boss. I come back in an hour.

In Germany it is not like Britain, where you go into a shop and you ask for advice and they haven't a clue. If you go to a building supply store the people working there will know all about the different grades of wood. If you go to a shop that sells beds the people working there will know all about the construction of the beds, and which beds are good for the back, and the beds are all really well built because people know what they're doing. And if you go to a haberdashers the staff will know all about the different types of cloth, and the proper thread to use, and the proper zip to use with a particular weight of cloth, and if you try to buy the wrong thing they will be really strict. So it is holding back the economy because to get a certain sort of job you have to have had this training, but if you go into a shop they are knowledgeable. So Adalberto was the one who was so keen on this project but he was doing it in this impulsive Italian way which would never come out right, because to do it right, look, here was the *shopkeeper* who had been *working in the trade* since her teens, and Adalberto wanted to rely on the memory of someone who did an apprenticeship back in *1962*.

So you have to love this about the Italians, that they are completely impulsive and unpredictable and inconsistent, and in the War they were not at all keen to exterminate the Jews, after the Germans occupied France Jews would go to *Italy* to escape the Vichy regime, and that is what you have to love about them. And if you look at Goethe, if you look at Germans who love the South, you see that is what they do love about it, that love of the moment.

But if you are going to do something properly you have to plan ahead or you will end up cutting the moment wrong. Then events will be all wrinkled and puckered.

She had brought the suit with her because if you are buying notions you can't rely on memory. So now she brought it out of the bag and she explained that her friend wanted more like it, and maybe it would be quite hard because it was made in 1962. And then she told this little lie, because if she told the truth it would sound completely bonkers. She said she thought maybe he was making a movie and he wanted the costumes to be authentic. This would be something that a German would understand, that you would want the details to be correct.

The saleswoman looked at the suit. She said: Did you make this?

She said: Yes: a long time ago.

She had not been back to Germany since she left. After the years of hitchhiking she had gone to Britain, because if she would go to Germany she would kill herself. It was as if she had discontinued German, and then had to dig up a tube of it at the back of a cupboard.

The woman was looking at the suit, inspecting the workmanship and nodding and making little noises of appreciation. She said she thought she had something that would work.

She brought out this bolt of cloth that nobody would ever have picked up for something to wear. If you would make a suit in it the suit would last for a million years. It was this muddy olive green.

The woman said: Does he want different colours?

If you set out to make something ugly it is like setting out to make something beautiful, you will just end up with kitsch.

So she had to pretend she was just making some suits the way they used to make suits.

They had two kinds of grey, a navy blue, a dull mustardy tan, a black, two kinds of brown, and then the linings. There was a chest with 25 drawers, and on 5 of the drawers was a button. That was the selection of buttons. There were those metal zips that nobody uses any more.

You could see the shop had been there since before the War, so its fittings were unchanged. The chest of drawers for the buttons had remained unchanged, but production of buttons would have been suspended during the War, *luxury* buttons, and under the

Communists this would not have been a high priority, the resumption of button production. After the Wall fell dressmaking would maybe not look sexy so the shop would not be rushing to expand. So there was something touching about the 5 buttons, it made you want to buy them, but to do the suit properly you would cover buttons in the same cloth, to show your skill.

And this was another thing that was quite old-fashioned, the shop had the linen that used to be used for the interface. It used to be you would use linen for the interface, and you would *sew* it in under the collar using these big stitches, *basting*, now they have an artificial material, and you can even iron it on, but in the east maybe they would be more conservative so this was this shop in 1992.

Adalberto came back. He looked at what was on the counter and he said OK, but we take the whole cloth because maybe they stop making it.

If the collar of a suit is to fall properly the inside, the underside has to be smaller than the outside. So you have to *mould* the cloth to shape it properly. There is a special stand of wood, with a wooden crossbar covered in padding, and you hang the jacket on it, and then you can work on it with an iron. It is not all sewing, there is a lot you can do with heat. But you need proper equipment. So they did not find this in Leipzig but they went to Berlin and bought one and it was a nightmare to get on the plane, but if you are flying first class they are more friendly and helpful, even the Germans. You would have thought Adalberto was their long-lost uncle, everyone was so anxious to help with the stand and the bolts of cloth.

So Adalberto was going to New York and he said he would like to do a show in 2 months.

When you make a garment for the Geselle you have one week to do it under exam conditions. You can't ask anyone how to do something. The room is all set up with the equipment, and you go in from 7 to 6, and you work there. But that was one week for one suit at the end of three years of hell, when you can do it all in your sleep. And the cutting has already been done for you, because you learn to make the pattern and cut in the next stage, that is when you start being creative. So even if there are some things that are more mechanical to talk of doing 19 suits in 2 months, single-handed, was mad. But if you would pour cold water on the idea of someone like Adalberto he would not find a way around the problem, or give you another month, he would just lose interest and do something else.

People think it would be easy to walk away.

Artists are lucky to get a gallerist, and you think if you get a gallerist the world is your oyster, and then maybe you are still teaching or working in a call centre. But if Charles Saatchi would walk into the gallery and buy out the show, or walk into the studio and buy out the studio, you would not have to worry any more. There are these collectors who can make a career. And there are these gallerists that people watch, they can make a career. So you know if you tell one to go away because he is interested in something that doesn't interest you, probably you will never meet someone like that again.

On the weekend of the open studio the administrator was already writing to her for the third time about the rent. But naturally word got round about Adalberto. If you think that the people who run it are *dreaming* that someone like Adalberto will just *come*, and that if he would take up an artist they would be over the moon, they are not going to throw out that artist because of the rent. But if they would hear that it is all off they would be hounding you for a cheque.

The paintings on the walls were defenceless. They could not dry faster if it would not be possible to pay the rent on the studio.

The paint is completely trusting. You think if nobody else is going to look after it it is up to you.

She had a superstition. If you have made your Gesellenstück, you should not let it go. So she made 20 new suits, instead of 19, and this was a very clever thing to do.

If you watch art auctions maybe you will think there are some very rich artists, because Hockney's *Portrait of Nick Wilder* sold for £3 million. But Hockney sold the painting a long time ago. It is the paintings from the 60s and 70s that make that money, and it is the people who own those paintings, and the people who handle the sale, who make the money. So it is too bad for Hockney that he did not keep aside a painting from that time.

Nobody would ask Hockney, at least you think nobody would ask Hockney to go back to that early style. You think he must have enough money so he would not be pressurised, anyway. But what if somebody discovers what you were doing in 1962, and they commission you to do 19 more of what you were doing in 1962? If you can do even one you can do 19, and if you can do 19 you can do 20.

So she did 20, and Adalberto never saw her Gesellenstück again, because it stayed on its padded hanger.

Adalberto gave her a cheque for £45,000, because he had subtracted the cost of the materials. So he had made this really grand gesture of wanting to buy out the shop, but if he would have done it she would have had to pay for all that useless stuff, and she *still* had bolts and bolts of material.

If you have followed the British art scene at all you will know that there are some things that are secondary. Tracey Emin made a tent called *Everyone I Have Ever Slept With* and the point was not the quality of the stitching. Later Emin did some other sewn work, but she got other people to do the sewing, and Hirst's dot paintings were not executed by Hirst, and this is all in the tradition of Warhol's Factory.

This would not do for Adalberto. It was the hatefulness of the pockets, the pleats, the buttonholes, the hatefulness of the stitching, that gave the garment its brutality. How is a garment to be brutal if made by someone lucky to get the work?

So Adalberto came back from New York, and he walked up and down in front of the 20 suits. They had been pressed with a proper steam iron. These were the wallflowers.

He said: What is that German word? Schrecklich.

He hung the 20 hideous suits in his showroom in Milan. The show could never be so transgressive outside Milan—if you have no sense of style, if you know nothing of design, you cannot *see* the stupidity of the ugly pocket which only a trained apprentice could execute correctly. But in Milan they practically fainted. Miuccia Prada bought out the show.

Adalberto still wanted to have a show in New York. Prada said OK.

Adalberto did not like the kind of catalogue that gives a cv of the artist.

Adalberto did not like it when an image of the artist was used as a sign of the artist.

Adalberto came to talk to her. He said: We are doing a show in New York. It's not Italy, they are not so sophisticated, people need things spelled out.

He said: I need a, what is the word, urine sample.

He had one of those little plastic cups, and you know, maybe you think it is for a visa or something, so she went to the loo.

Adalberto said: That's great and we will need one of the other, here is a box for it,

and she *knew* she would have heard of it if the US government made people give a shit sample,

she said: Adalberto, what are you doing?

Adalberto said: We are doing a show in New York. We have to be more explicit. That's all.

He said: It's about the body. Hatred of the body. Denial of the body. The hanging requires the body.

He said: I hate the kind of hanging where you have seen it a million times, the lighting is a cliché, the frames are a cliché, and then the buyer wants to know if it comes with the fucking frame and you want to say sure, and just for you we are throwing in a free pack of underwear autographed by the artist, I hate that crap.

Adalberto said Prada said she would maybe show it in the store in Tokyo.

That was because of the purity of the idea of the urine sample. People have this idea of the frame, a piece of wood, a piece of metal contiguous with the piece, we really have to get away from that.

Adalberto said: Now don't freak out on me.

He said: Are you still menstruating?

If you go to some new country you think you can leave behind the universe of words you grew up with, and even in the new country people are always building that cage of words, that is why it is good that art can be a thing. But people are always thinking they can break through the cage another way. When she was in art school in the 70s it was this very radical experimental time and sometimes people would do art that the teachers did not get, there was this bloke who did an installation in Manchester or it might have been Bradford and he had the examiners come out for it, and they just left. So he didn't get a degree. And even in those days it was funny that art was supposed to be transgressive but you were supposed to get a degree, but to be an artist and not go to art school would have been the absolute pits. But it was exciting because these famous artists would come to talk to the students, or you could go to London and see the shows and it was all happening right now.

There was this guy, Kerry Trengrove, he died, he smoked and he drank, if you do both it's bad, he got cancer of the throat and tongue. Most of his stuff ended up in the skip. But he did groundbreaking work. He did a show at Covent Garden, they put on very new things, he dug this deep hole in the ground of the gallery, just big enough to sleep and move around in. And he put a bed in, and a wall of Complan, and he covered it over with thick glass, with just enough of a gap to let air in, and he stayed there a week, he did everything there, he slept and ate and peed, and people could come and look down and see him underground. And that was groundbreaking work. That was back in the 70s. And he did another piece, he got these dogs, that were disturbed, or strays, and he stayed with them in a room for a week, and just by being there with him, for the week, they became tame.

And now, who has heard of Kerry Trengrove? Maybe five other people.

Or this other artist, Stuart Brisley. He was *the* performance artist in the 70s. He got this bath and he filled it full of offal and he lay in it. Another time he went on the roof of the Hayward Gallery, and he had himself strung up, naked, upside down. First he covered himself in this thick clay mud—his work always had this painterly quality—and then he had himself strung up, and it was already autumn so it was quite cold, and someone stood on the ground with a hose and hosed him down—*cleansed* him.

But *he* is in books. You can read about him in books. So there is a record. That is why records are so important. You need someone to be there, to be a witness.

But all that expressiveness, that confessionality, that exhibitionism, that plastering of more meaning on the world, maybe you want to leave that, maybe you just do.

But then maybe you think of the paintings going in a skip. Maybe you think if someone wants to be a witness for this kind of covert exhibitionism then the paintings will not go in the skip.

This was this very bad time when the National Gallery was quite keen on plastering meaning on its collections, so once a year they would have an exhibition and a big banner outside the National Gallery that said Making and Meaning, and if she would take a bus through Trafalgar Square she would want to vomit, the buses through Trafalgar Square should have art sickness bags during the Making and Meaning Season but they didn't.

And now here was Adalberto with this idea that he was a curative genius and if other people got that idea all the gallerists would be doing it.

But maybe you don't see this, if you have done something you were never going to do again and somebody asks you to do something else you would not really do it is easy to go down that road.

Adalberto said if she was not menstruating they would just take a blood sample with a syringe but it would not be so good. He said they were going to have to use someone else for the breast milk which was not so good.

Sometimes the fact that something is easy seduces you. It is not like making a buttonhole or a pleat, the body is producing these fluids and solids and it is so simple to collect them.

Adalberto took her to this gym as a guest member, what a production. Men today have these bodies that you never used to see, they are pouring these hours into the body, if you look at Jim Morrison that is the type of body that men used to have and a man with a body like Anthony Quinn in *La Strada* would be really embarrassing because it would be really over the top, but today nobody would want a body like Anthony Quinn because it would not be buff. Compared to what men have nowadays that would be nothing, and here was Adalberto with one of these bodies, and he was saying she must wear 3 sweatshirts and 2 pairs of sweatpants and run on a treadmill but it was not practical to run because she had been poor for so long. So he said OK, and he punched this button until the track was quite steep. He had brought this motorcycle helmet that he put on her head. It had a little rubber cup where the chin strap was and he said he would be back in 15 minutes.

It took about an hour to collect the sweat.

He said she could use an onion for the tears.

He said if he gave her a cup she could spit into it.

He said maybe she could get really drunk so they could get the vomit.

If you have never been there you think it is easy to walk away.

She went to New York for the show. She flew first class. They put her up at this posh hotel called Morgan's.

When she saw the show it was not as bad as she thought. On one side of the room, on one long wall, were the suits. On the facing wall there were these tiny shelves, maybe 4 cm by 4 cm, in aluminium, and on each shelf was a glass container with thick sides flush with the edges of the shelf, and in this container would be the piss or the sweat or the blood, so it did have its beauty. It was good that there was this vast space between the work of art and the frame, you know when something is curated there is this mania for attaching things to it, words, facts, there will be a little card on the wall and people will go anxiously to the card to avail themselves of its wisdom and return to the work of art with the little trophy, these words that were on the card, and sometimes you will see people hunting manically for the card—

So there was a boldness about this space that was good, and it was good having the works of art on one wall somehow, and the numbers were by the glass jars on the opposite wall and there was nothing on the wall with the works of art at all. So that was quite clever and mischievous.

Maybe if you are making art that is a thing, maybe if that thinginess is what you immerse yourself in, if you spend all that time away from about, if you are never attaching, maybe you are lost to words after a while, then someone comes along who is really good at manipulating and you can't make words push for you.

But maybe it is just that Italians are slippery. In the War the Nazis would send directives to the Italians about extraditing Jews and they could not get them to cooperate. The Italians could not get excited about it and if they are not excited about it they are not going to do it but if they are excited about it you can't stop them.

The papers had said that Prada had bought out the show for $1 million. Maybe it wasn't true. She would rehearse things to say to Adalberto but he was quite hard to pin down.

Then one day it was in the papers that an artist had had him declared bankrupt. If someone doesn't pay you this is something you can do, have them declared bankrupt. This artist had been quite clever, she had a contract and that was what made it possible to recover the debt. But all the other artists he owed money did not have contracts. There was nothing on paper to give them a right. And anyway he was a limited company.

So the £45,000 was all that was left from the 20 suits, and some of it had to go to the Inland Revenue. So the only thing was to do a show while that excitement was still in the air.

This was really tricky because Serge did not want to be abandoned but he felt somehow he had been left with the less interesting work, it poisoned his interest in the painting. Serge wanted her to make some more suits for the London gallery. He was desperate to be cutting edge. If he would show suits all the bigwigs in London would come because they did not see them in Milan and New York. But it had been happening for so long that a lot of the paintings were really really dry. So she said he could show *one suit* if he would do a show for the paintings, but it would not be for sale.

So Serge had this show. And naturally now he nominated her for the Turner. Anybody can make a nomination but because of Adalberto she made the shortlist. They invited her to submit a piece, and sometimes you get disgusted. You keep thinking the tide will turn and painting will stop being unfashionable and then it would be exciting to be shortlisted for the Turner. But the Turner selects these things that are exciting for people who don't know anything about art. In art school there is someone in every year doing minimalism, or conceptualism, and then the Turner will pick somebody who is doing what people do in their first year of art school, so it is kind of disgusting to get selected. So then Serge was saying I'm not saying another *word*. My lips are *sealed*. You *know* what I think, but I'm not putting *any pressure* on you, because it's absolutely your decision.

And maybe you would think that this would be the big chance to show what interests you. But the thing about being an artist is that from the minute you go to art school you realise there is this need to be canny. There is this need to make a name for yourself. There is this need to deal with the people who have the power. And Turner, Turner did it as much as anybody, he was a genius but he did what he had to do to get into the Royal Academy. So when she applied for UK citizenship it was not just a rejection of Germany. Why would she do it if not to be eligible for the Turner if the chance would come? So if you have set it up to give yourself that chance, there is this obvious next step to do, give them what you think they will want to win. And she was really tired and anxious because of Adalberto going bankrupt, and the cut-off age was 50 so this was this last year she would be eligible, and sometimes a story has a momentum of its own, and it was as if they had nominated a puppet. So she submitted her Gesellenstück, and the way she installed it was she hung it on one wall under a white light, and on the opposite wall, down the long end of the room, she put a glass jar of spermicidal jelly.

My Heart Belongs to Bertie

Let's take 2 people, A and B. A is a heroin addict. B's idea of a narcotic is Earl Grey tea.

We take a randomly selected infant, toss a coin, and allocate it according to the result of the coin toss: Heads A, Tails B.

We repeat the procedure.

In 10 trials, the likeliest number of Heads is 5. If we run sequences of 10 trials, though, we shall sometimes have fewer than 5, sometimes more, and the distribution of Heads will follow the familiar Gaussian curve:

In 20 trials, the likeliest number of "successes" is 10—that is, the Gaussian curve shifts to the right:

AUTHOR'S NOTE: Many years ago a friend commented that we rarely see fiction that shows the way mathematicians think. He talked about the styles of play in poker of a mathematician, an economist and a philosopher. The thing that struck me as especially interesting was the different ways of thinking about probability; I was a great admirer of Edward Tufte's work on information design, and I thought this might be used in some way to make non-intuitive ways of thinking about probability visible on the page.

I began reading obsessively about statistics and probability. Peter Bernstein's *Against the Gods: The Remarkable Story of Risk* was one inspiration; he says: "The revolutionary idea that defines the boundary between modern times and the past is the mastery of risk: the notion that the future is more than a whim of

The two PDFs lodged awkwardly upside down at Peter's edge of the table, jamming up against napkin dispenser, sugar pourer, salt & pepper shakers, red plastic bottle of ketchup, yellow plastic bottle of mustard.

When one gives a lecture or seminar, one does not have to do battle with condiments. He had not prepared for the contingency.

If we repeat the procedure on a daily basis, said Peter, ineffectually shifting the PDFs to give Jim a better view, the infant's exposure to misallocation will tend to be rectified with relative frequency—though, on the other hand, the infant will never be guaranteed enjoyment of a good draw for very long. If the procedure is conducted weekly, more hangs on the result; if monthly, quarterly, yearly, more still.

He pressed the palms of his hands to his eyes.

Peter had written a book of robot tales with a happy beginning which had made, as it turned out, what seemed a lot of money, and yet not enough money to mitigate contractual relations with

---

the gods and that men and women are not passive before nature." Analysis of probability seemed more compelling than ever for fiction; I spent endless hours grappling with R, a programming language with strength in statistical graphics.

R is open source, and it has come a long way since I first downloaded the DMG.

What hasn't changed, I think, is the gap between people who see why understanding chance matters and people who just don't get it—people who don't see why this is crucial to the most basic questions of ethics. I have more glamorous plots in my portfolio than the primitive efforts on display in this story, but the philosophical issue was what I hoped to bring into the open.

persons who had professed to love it yet sought to remove references to $e^{i\pi}$. He had *explained* that discovering $e^{i\pi}$ at the age of 9 was the only thing that had kept him from *suicide* and been brushed indulgently aside.

The money had appeared to make it worth the while of Jim (said to be a "hot shot literary agent") to represent Peter's interests on a second book of robot tales. It had proved more complicated than had first appeared.

Jim did not know the secret of a happy beginning: My parents died when I was born.

Peter had made a special trip to New York to explain the binomial distribution in person to Jim. He wanted to reduce the likelihood of contractual obligation to persons like the persons he knew too well.

Now they sat in a booth in a diner.

Peter had suggested meeting in Jim's flat, on the assumption that this would minimise the number of people in the vicinity mistakable for Jim.

Jim had held out for the diner.

Peter had suggested that Jim wear a yellow sweater for ease of identification.

Jim had not taken up the suggestion.

Jim was wearing a brown pullover and brown trousers. His hair and eyes were brown. For the whole of the walk from office to diner Peter had been terrified of losing sight of Jim in the crowd and then failing to recognise him again. The worry now was that if, for instance, Jim went to the men's room and someone else came and sat down, Peter might fail to notice the difference. That was one worry, and another worry was that the name "Jim" might slip his mind, as names generally did.

The surface of the table was taken up with all sorts of paraphernalia superfluous, not to say impedimental, to ratiocination. Peter had done what he could to maximise the surface area available for display of illustrative materials; he had waived the offer of lunch. Jim had ordered something or other. He had exchanged badinage with the waitress.

We posit daily reassignment, Peter went doggedly on. As our number of trials approaches 100, the number of days of infant allocation to A comes to cluster, of course, around 50:

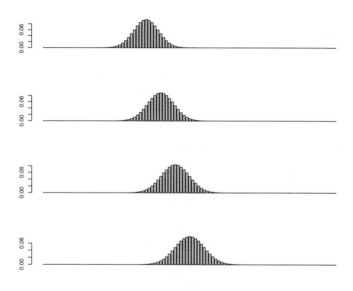

He had been up all night running variations in R on

```
par(mfrow=c(3,1))
barplot(dbinom(0:100,10,.5))
barplot(dbinom(0:100,20,.5))
barplot(dbinom(0:100,30,.5))
```

—all this before catching the 5 am AirBus to Gatwick from Gloucester Green, Oxford's answer to Port Authority. In his haste he had, he realised, forgotten to label the x axis.

He would have liked, at this point, to throw in the towel, or rather retreat to his hotel and address the issue of the unlabelled x axis. But they were here. One must make the most of it.

Jim squirted ketchup placidly on crinkled fries. It seemed unlikely that a properly labelled x axis would have made the thing usefully clearer.

Perhaps Jim was one of the lucky ones. If he was an orphan he probably had all kinds of rosy notions.

But in *fact*, of course, persevered Peter—he had really been talking, understand, for only a minute or so, in a lecture he could have talked uninterrupted for an *hour*, with *hand-outs*, a *blackboard*—50% of adults are not heroin addicts, so a model with a 50:50 chance of drawing one isn't a very good fit. Suppose we try to get a feel for uneven odds.

You see, I suppose, that we can imagine a pool of 10 parents with 1 heroin addict and 9 tea-drinkers, or a pool with 9 heroin addicts and 1 tea-drinker. Instead of tossing a coin we draw, perhaps, a ball from an urn (containing, as it might be, 1 black ball 9 white or 9 black balls 1 white) and replace it before the next draw. In the first instance, over one *hundred* trials, the number of As—that is, draws of a heroin addict—would cluster around 10,

whereas in the second instance it would cluster around 90.

So the *point* is, on our model of daily draws, the likelihood of drawing a heroin addict 90 days out of 100 arises only with a pool of 9 heroin addicts and 1 tea-drinker: it does *not* arise when only 1 in 10 possible parents is a heroin addict, and by extension would be even *less* likely in a population where only 1 in 100,000 was an addict. (According to Heyman, in a recent national, that is to say American, survey, there were in fact about 3.4 opiate addicts per thousand persons and about 10.8 nonaddicted heavy users.) *Whereas*, under the current system, even if only 1 in 100,000 is an addict, the fact that all depends on a single draw, the accident of birth, means that a child born to such a person is assigned 365 days out of 365 until the age of majority.

The point is simply, said Peter, that the family is a barbarous institution. One *is*, for the most part, stuck with the luck of a single draw.

Oh, families, said Jim. I *know*, I *know*, I *know*.

He took a healthy swallow from his glass of Diet Coke and set it down.

Look, said Jim. This is fascinating, but it's way over my head. I don't really get it all, but I don't *need* to get it.

Jim put his plate unhurriedly to one side, rested his forearms on the table and laced his fingers together, with a quiet mastery of the space that—that is, if Jim had been the one who had wanted to present PDFs displaying the binomial distribution, an army of ketchup bottles would not have stood in his way.

You're a very brilliant guy, said Jim. *You're* the genius. You found a way to capture the imagination of a lot of kids who would not normally go for this stuff. You captured the imagination of a lot of adults who wouldn't normally read books for kids. So if you want to talk about the odds, maybe I'm in a better position to know the kinds of odds you were beating. I'm in a better position to know why this is very exciting to a lot of other people who understand the kind of odds you were beating. What I can say is that a lot of people are very excited by your work; I know a lot of editors who would love to see a new book. So this would be a very good time to send something out, have an auction. Bottom line, if we don't get a significant six-figure deal it's time for me to take up knitting, and if we play our cards right we could be talking low seven.

Jim had already explained, by e-mail, that the option on Peter's second book, held by the lucky publisher of Peter's first book (advance: £5,000; sales: 500,000), was not an obstacle. The book must be *submitted* first to the lucky publisher, but if their offer was unsatisfactory Peter (or, rather, Peter's agent on his behalf) was entitled to submit the book elsewhere.

This was, obviously, an improvement on our barbarous domestic arrangements: a parent does not have an *option* on a child, and the terms of the relationship do not come up for renegotiation. Peter's position—and the reason for this ill-starred trip to New York—was that the objection to the lucky publisher was not financial. The objection was that it had done its best to dilute elements of the book likely to appeal to the underserved numerate, and to put off the innumerate who were already, one might have thought, amply provided for, an example being the hideous war of attrition it had waged over inclusion of $e^{i\pi}$.

The fact that Jim could unashamedly admit to finding a *perfectly simple explanation* of the *binomial distribution* over his head, that he could unblushingly dismiss it as the province of genius, only went to show how deep-seated innumeracy actually is in our benighted culture. (If an *agent*, a 'hot shot', who notionally represents a client's financial interests, can be functionally innumerate—!!!) But how could he possibly do battle with ignorance if he himself—

By the time a boy is 10 he has spent 3,652 days under governance of the allocation of a single draw. There's nothing to be done about it. All the more reason not to enter into contractual relations lightly.

It's unreasonable, perhaps, to expect someone like Jim to understand the full horror.

Exactly, said Peter. (Meet the man on his own ground.) *Exactly.* This is the whole beauty of business relations: we leave barbarity behind. Let us suppose I know about Merovingian kings; I wish either to work with someone with comparable knowledge of the Merovingians or, perhaps, to work with someone whose knowledge of the Carolingians supplements my relative ignorance of the period. We see at once that I should be highly unlikely to find a match leaving the matter to chance, but the invisible hand is my friend: I can pay for the information or, aliter visum, the value of the match enables all concerned to maximise profits regardless of whether money changes hands. Let us say no one with relevant knowledge can be found. Perhaps someone happens to know about the Dutch Tulip Bubble, and I discover in myself a hitherto unguessed-at interest in the Dutch Tulip Bubble. I can order my preferences, you know, in a way which is wholly out of the question in a family setting. As it *happens*, I have written a second book on robots and would like an editor with relevant expertise; if none can be found with expertise relevant to the book in hand, I would happily write a book relevant to such expertise as can be had. I rely on you to *brief* me so that I can make a rational decision.

Jim said he didn't work that way. Look, he said, we could waste a lot of time talking about editors. We're only interested in the ones who are willing to buy the book we have to sell. Once we have a list of serious contenders we can definitely talk about who would be best for the book.

As a child Peter had not been *unduly*, he wouldn't have said, troubled by the shortcomings of his parents per se. The thing that had bothered him was the fact that all *other* adults colluded in placing him in the largely unchecked power of these individuals. *All* adults, even the apparently decent ones, were in collusion with evil.

He had worked it out when he was, perhaps, 7 and never forgotten. That was why he was able to write for children. He was 35, a bad age.

Peter said, Please.

He tried to think of the sort of thing Americans say.

He said, It would mean a lot to me to work with someone who admired Bertrand Russell.

He said, It would really mean a lot to me.

The statement seemed, if not meaningless, then uselessly imprecise.

(The first book had made all this money. Why could he not use the money to buy what he wanted? Was that not the general point of having money in the first place?)

He said, I'd be happy to switch the percentages round if that would help. You'd be very welcome to take an 85% commission.

This was undoubtedly precise but was perhaps not the sort of thing Americans say. Jim said he was happy with the normal 15% commission.

Peter pressed the palms of his hands to his eyes.

Russell, he said presently.

Russell was born in 1872. His father, Viscount Amberley, was an atheist and Utilitarian; he asked John Stuart Mill to be godfather to the child. Russell's mother died when he was 2, his father when he was 4. His father's will appointed two atheists to be guardians to Russell and his brother, and stipulated that the children be raised as agnostics. Russell's grandmother, the Countess Russell, overturned the will and won guardianship of the children. She raised Russell on strictly religious principles. At the age of 11 he was introduced to geometry by his brother Frank; he said he had not imagined there was anything so beautiful in the world. He said later that only the desire to know more about mathematics restrained him from suicide.

I do understand, Peter said wearily, that we can't reasonably expect to find an editor of children's books with mathematical, scientific, or even philosophical training. But Russell, after all, was a great populariser; it's surely not beyond the realm of probability that a general reader should be familiar with his *popular* work, work *written* for a general audience. The thing that matters is not, ultimately, an understanding of number theory, or the structure of the atom, or the semantic tradition, but an unswerving commitment to the pursuit of truth. I should be happy to forgo 70% of the revenue from a book to avoid entrusting it to a person to whom this is perfectly indifferent; one has to be particularly scrupulous in these matters when writing for children. That is the overriding interest which I hope to persuade you to represent. As ours is a business relationship, a financial incentive cannot, it seems to me, be offensive as it would be among mathematicians, scientists or philosophers. It is entirely reasonable for me to determine my own ends and offer financial compensation to you for the inconvenience of promoting them.

Jim made a number of friendly American remarks. It was by no means clear that the offer of a financial inducement within the context of a business relationship had not been perceived as offensive. It was, unfortunately, painfully obvious that he had not warmed to the style of social interaction which is a robot's principal source of appeal. The business of adapting a robot to American manners is, of course, an engineering feat of considerable ambition.

Peter said, Will you excuse me a minute?

He stood up and left the diner.

In Oxford he was able to smoke at the Union, to which his father had given him a life membership in his freshman year.

He drifted to the lee of a wall. He took out a packet of Dunhills and lit one.

As a child he had had five imaginary robots as friends.

The robots had stopped talking to him somewhere during the protracted battles over $e^{i\pi}$. It was a happy accident that a second book had been finished before they stopped talking.

It seemed unlikely that intervention from Jim would bring the robots back.

Perhaps Jim *was* an orphan.

Peter stubbed out his Dunhill on the sole of his shoe. He slipped it into a pocket. He pressed the palms of his hands to his eyes.

At his shoulder he heard a voice he had not heard for some time.

The robot pointed out pleasantly, dispassionately, that it would, certainly, be political suicide for a legislator to attempt to introduce an aleatory element into the allocation of minors, but that this was far from exhausting possible solutions. Research had already demonstrated that autistic children responded well to robot companions. It was only a matter of time before a robot companion was seen as an effective developmental adjunct for every child. From this it was a short step to recognition of the fact that each child would best be served by a complement of robotic aides. Robots could be exchanged, upgraded, used in different combinations with none of the social constraints affecting human subjects.

That's true, said Peter.

He propped his right shoulder against the wall, right leg loosely bent, left leg perhaps 20 degrees from the perpendicular, left hand shoved in a pocket.

The robot observed that, as all children would be guaranteed a minimum of one rational companion, exposure to the variable rationality of the human beings in whose charge a child found itself would be significantly limited in the damage it could do.

Peter did not say anything, for he was listening attentively. His gaze had fallen to the ground as the least troublesome place for it.

The robot continued to speak. It was restful in the way that robots are restful.

When a human being develops an argument, when a human being attempts not only to think but to speak with precision, he or she is often made to feel that this is a mark of social inadequacy and that there is something comical about it. The younger the human being, the more humorous it becomes. So that humans whose inclination it is to think and speak in this way become self-conscious from an early age, and a kind of minstrelisation creeps in.

It was once the case that so-called minstrel shows were put on for the amusement of white audiences, and for these *blacks* would *black up*, put on *black-face* (!!!!!!!), exaggerating what whites perceived as comically grotesque features of negroid appearance, exchanging dialogue exaggerating what whites perceived as the ignorance and stupidity of the inferior race. In a similar way the rationalist is socialised to mug for the camera, trotting out recondite facts, objecting to logical fallacies, using polysyllabic words in sentences with a high number of dependent clauses, with the quizzical air of one who knows he is amusing the interlocutor by conforming to a fondly held stereotype.

A robot lacks this self-consciousness; one becomes aware of one's own seeing the robot's lack. A robot is, in any case, a machine: if it *were* conscious it would know that machines are not socially stigmatised for sounding like machines. A man who is accustomed to social stigma tends, curiously enough, to be repelled by persons like himself who are tarred with the same social stigma; it is a comfort to talk to a robot, in which rationality carries no stigma.

Peter lit another Dunhill while the robot talked persuasively on.

Ah! the revivifying properties of tobacco! Peter remembered suddenly that in his hour of need, viz. 3 am Greenwich Mean Time, he had fired off an e-mail to Andrew Gelman, Director of Applied Statistics at Columbia University, entreating assistance. If he had not been relatively new to R he would undoubtedly have known what to do; if he had not been catching the AirBus at 5 am he could undoubtedly have worked it out; these are *not* the circumstances in which one goes to the R Help Forum and exposes one's ignorance to Brian Ripley, Duncan Murdoch, Gabor Grothendieck, Uwe Ligges, Peter Dalgaard, Deepayan Sarkar and other R supremos. Professor Gelman, on the other hand, had a son who had liked the first robot book; at 3 am the circumstance had seemed to extenuate.

At this very moment a reply to his e-mail might be waiting! He had spotted a Staples and a Kinko's on 6th Avenue; either, surely, would permit him to see if anything useful had come in. Or for that matter—His laptop was in his hotel room. And his hotel (chosen for proximity to a bar at which one was permitted to smoke) was just off 8th Avenue, which was, he *rather* thought, just around the corner. (No longer a penniless academic, he had been easily able to afford the rates of the Gansevoort.)

Peter strode purposefully off—nothing like talking to a robot for clearing the head!

Restored, presently, to the comforts of the Gansevoort, he opened his trusty laptop, and what to his wondering eyes should appear but an e-mail from Andrew Gelman, his *friend*.

Dear Peter,

I'm not exactly sure what you're looking for, but here's my quick try:

```
n <- c (10, 20, 50, 90, 100)
n.graphs <- length (n)
par (mfrow=c(n.graphs,1), mar=c(2,2,0,1),
  mgp=c(1.5,.5,0), tck=-.01)
total <- 70
for (i in 1:n.graphs){
```

```
barplot (dbinom(0:total,n[i],.5), width=1,
  space=0,xlim=c(0,total+1), ylim=c(0,.3),
  xaxs="i", yaxs="i", yaxt="n")
ticks <- seq (0, 200, 10)
axis (1, ticks+.5, ticks)
axis (2, c(0,.1,.2))
text (total-5, .2, paste ("(n = ", n[i], ")",
  sep=""), cex=1.2)
}
```

Peter launched R. He typed in the suggested code, and lo! a plot appeared, a beautiful little array of histograms with the *x axis labelled*!

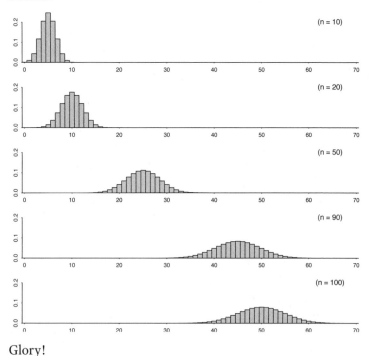

Glory!

He dashed off an e-mail to Gelman expressing his undying

gratitude. Gift horse and all that, he could not *quite* see why the x axis ended at 70: an odd choice given that, when number of draws n=100, 0–37 and 63–100 are in fact symmetrical gaps—would one not want the symmetry to be visible? (But then he could not quite remember what he had said at the dark hour of 3 am.)

He scrutinized the code, yes, yes, yes, it was a simple matter of changing total to 100, and one might also, perhaps, want to have n in *all* multiples of 10 up to 100? Hey presto!

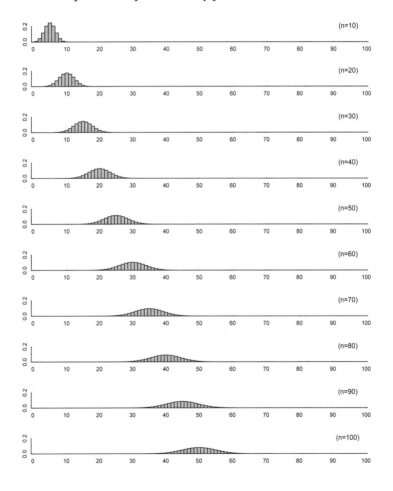

There's an experience that's common enough. One picks up a book, begins to read. When one looks up 5 hours have passed. One sits in a cold train on a siding; snow falls softly on a stubbled field.

5 hours later Peter found himself in a Korean diner flanked by 5 robots.

One of the robots was talking about Clovis, who ascended the throne at the age of 15.

It's important to be rational.

Correlation is not causation, no. But what is to be done? What he has to go on is that, after a gap of over a year, all five robots had started talking again after this *extraordinarily* kind, helpful and above all elegant solution from Andrew Gelman, *exactly* the sort of assistance he might have hoped to find in a competent editor. But if, for the sake of argument, a book is worth a significant six figures or low seven, and if, for the sake of argument, a book depends in the first instance on being in communication with the robots, we can *quantify* the value of working with a Gelman-equivalent. But the *first* robot had spoken after he walked out of the

diner!!!!!!!!! *Jim*!!!!!!!!! There had been a man named *Jim*—

Ought he, perhaps, to go rushing back to, oh God, the other

But no, Jim (he was *pretty* sure it was Jim) would have gone back to his office. Ought he, in all decency, to drop off the correctly labelled chart at the office? Or call, perhaps he should

There was the matter of the briefcase, but it had only contained print-outs of PDFs which were on the laptop, so there was no *particular* need to retrieve, but

Wait. Wait wait wait wait wait wait wait.

As we were *saying*, before we were so *rudely* interrupted, the first robot made its presence known after one had walked out on Jim. We are unhappily not in the position of being able to run randomised blind trials. We can only proceed, with the utmost caution, on the evidence available.

A *tentative* conclusion is that there are compelling *financial,* as well as *intellectual,* reasons to abstain from communication with Jim. (Note that Jim had strictly confined his contribution to the *financial element.*) There would *appear* to be compelling financial reasons to communicate with Andrew Gelman (his *friend*), except that the man is not on the payroll of an agency or publisher. *But.*

But but but but but.

Surely.

If he understands the matter correctly, the plucky underdog, his first publisher, inveterate enemy that it is of $e^{i\pi}$, can't compel him to give them the second book.

Is this not what is meant by leverage?

Can he *not*, in fact, make any deal conditional on exclusive consultation with his *friend* (at a suitable fee) or some suitably numerate and computerate substitute?

He *rather* thinks he *can.*

On the Town

Benny Bergsma didn't like to talk about his father, but people who had loved the *Automatika* series as children always wanted to hear about him. If the subject came up he did not know how to back away.

What he would say was that his father did not discuss the creative process.

He would say, if pushed: "If a contract has to be notarized he won't sign it." He was always pushed.

He would say, if pushed further: "If there's going to be a movie, he doesn't want to go to the premiere." He was always pushed further.

What it meant was that his Craigslist ad, offering thirty square feet of subprime real estate in Benny's loft in Dumbo, had to be reposted eight weeks in a row, while Benny sifted through the hundreds, nay thousands of applicants who proved, upon investigation, to have read and loved the *Automatika* series in their rugrat days. So the Boy from Iowa was a shoo-in. Gil had not read the *Automatika* series because it was not set in New York.

There are 7 billion people on the planet. Of these, a mere 17 million have the privilege of living in the New York Greater Metropolitan Area. If you want stories about people who don't live in New York, was his attitude, real *life* offers such stories in appalling abundance. And if you are one of the real lifers who happen not to be one of the 17 million, *reading* about New York is as close, pending a change of luck, as you are going to *get*. Why would you read a *book* set anywhere *else*?[1]

As a non-fan Gil had no interest in Jaap Bergsma per se, but rooming with the embittered alcoholic son of the author of a cult series, this is very New York. Very unIowa.

He paid the deposit by PayPal, turned up a week later with his backpack, unloaded it on the bed and headed back to Manhattan.

It was his first day in New York! And on his very first *day*, when he hadn't even un*packed*, he saw Harvey *Keitel* eating a pancake in a diner! A diner in the *Village*! Needless to say he immediately entered the diner, not to intrude on Mr. Keitel, obviously, but simply to order the identical pancake.

Gil checked the listings in *Time Out*. He had saved up a list of films that he wanted to see for the first time in New York (*Jules et Jim*; *Breathless*; *Battleship Potemkin*; *La Dolce Vita*; *Bicycle Thieves*; *The Leopard*; all of Kurosawa, Mizoguchi, Ozu, because if there is a *season* you want to be able to *immerse* yourself in the *oeuvre*), holding out, somehow, in the face of often almost irresistible temptation, till the age of 22.[2] And *now*, by an amazing piece of luck, *Jules et Jim* was showing at the Tribeca!!!!!

Five hours permitted a preliminary pancake-fueled exploration of the island before box office time.

---

1. Except, obviously, to avoid looking totally uneducated when you actually *get* to New York. Kafka, Borges, Proust—these you should read.

2. There was a second list of films which he had had to downgrade to "Okay to watch in Iowa," because he did not want to come to New York and look completely uneducated, but he had never felt good about it. He had mental conversations with an interlocutor who said "*Wild Strawberries*? Are you telling me *Wild Strawberries* doesn't deserve first-time-viewing-in-New-*York*? Are you *serious*?" to which Gil would mentally reply that it was not a question of the artistic *merit* of the film, on which, as someone who hadn't even *seen* it, he was unable to comment, but a question of what *felt* right for the viewing experience. That was the mental

Gil had never had any desire to go to France, he had simply wanted to watch French films in New *York*. And when he saw Jeanne Moreau, at last, declaiming "To be or not to be," he was glad he had waited. He was glad he had held out for something special.

He got back to the loft at ten p.m. or so. Benny was sitting crosslegged on a downtrodden sofa, morosely leafing through the *Wall Street Journal*.

Gil shared the glad tidings: "Dude!!!!!!!!!! I saw Harvey Keitel eating pancakes!!!!!!!!!"

Benny: "Huh."

It seemed best not to add to the man's misery by mentioning *Jules et Jim*.

"Want a beer?" asked Ben.

"Sure," said Gil. He felt slightly the worse for wear, truth be told, having been up since dawn the previous day, what with all the packing and discarding and fare-thee-welling not to mention actual traveling, not to mention the excitements of the day, but Iowans take their sociability seriously. He took a cold Sam Adams from the case in the fridge and joined Benny on the sofa. Benny lifted his beer-in-progress in downbeat cheer.

Benny, it quickly emerged, did not so much not want to talk about his father as not want to talk about anything else, the problem being, rather, that he did not like having to temper the wind to the shorn lamb.

"See, what *happened* is," said Benny, "my dad read a letter from

---

reply, but he felt bad about relegating *Bob le Flambeur*, *The Crow*, *La Ronde*, *Wings of Desire*, *La Strada*, *8½*, *Solaris*, plus much of Hitchcock, much of Mamet, all of Tarantino and others too numerous to mention to the Iowa League. He wished he had grown up in New York, so these invidious choices would not have been forced on him, but what was he to do?

The third list of films, obviously, was the list of films *set* in New York. But we digress.

45

Roald Dahl to Kingsley Amis saying write for kids, that's where the money is. So he *did*, and there *was*, it just wasn't *enough*."

The more money there was, the more thousands of nauseatingly cute letters or, more recently, e-mails poured in *from* kids, kids who imagined that world peace could be achieved if we all just sat down and popped popcorn together. Or swapped knock-knock jokes. Or played ping pong. Why can't we all just act like cute little kids?

A fifth of Jack Daniels into the day, Mr. Bergsma could not be guaranteed to ignore and discard. Dear Tommy, he would reply genially, Thank you for your interesting suggestion. I will pass the proposal on to Mr. Milosevic. Yours, J P Bergsma.

Only to get, meanwhile, in a mud- and bloodstained envelope, a heartrendingly charismatic letter from some kid whose whole family had been blown up when he was nine, a kid who had walked 500 miles through a warzone carrying only a battered copy of *Automatika* for comfort, a kid who had stowed away in a truck and now lived, *sans papiers*, on the streets of Paris, the whole couched in an uncomplaining stoicism, a nonchalant wit and erudition, which put the luckless Benny to shame. Mr. Bergsma would organize, at immense personal inconvenience and expense, a school, lawyer, bla. Doing irreparable damage to the personal fortune whose accumulation was the whole point of *writing* for kids in the *first* place.

The result being that *Benny* could never have music lessons, go to computer camp, go to private school, *anything.*

Gil could see why this might be somewhat disillusioning to fans of the series. While somewhat chilling and egotistical as such, anyway, though, it *was* the kind of thing he would definitely have expected of the embittered alcoholic son of the author of a cult series for kids. Very New York.

"Couldn't he hire someone?" he asked.

Benny said that his father's life was a ruined landscape of burned-out deals.

Gil would have been happy to crash at this point, but Benny, far from moving gracefully on, seemed to see a roommate as an economical substitute for a therapist.

Once, for instance, Benny elaborated, when Benny had just been accepted for admission at Choate, Jake Rabinowitz, a top entertainment lawyer, had negotiated a movie deal which included the right to two first-class tickets to the premiere.

Total dealbreaker.

Mr. Bergsma: "What is this. What the fuck is this."

JR: "I got them to agree to first-class tickets to the premiere."

Mr. Bergsma: "Look. I don't want this. I never asked for this. I don't want to clutter up my head with this crap."

JR: "The contract does not *require* you to attend the premiere."

Mr. Bergsma: "I don't want to get into all this crap about what I want or do not want. I am trying to *write* a fucking *book*. You have now used up *bargaining space*, you piece of shit, you have squandered *leverage*, for something about which I do not give a fuck. I want this out of the fucking contract. I want a Crap. Free. Deal."

Given that the whole issue of the premiere had been *raised*, given that it was not possible just to get on with the fucking book, given that it was *necessary* to discuss, Mr. Bergsma discussed the sort of thing he would have discussed had he chosen to discuss. But his lawyer, it evolved, would lose face if he went back to the other side with points the client actually cared about, such as fixing up a fixer-upper in Pittsburgh, rather than issues that were recognized as deal points by his industry peers.

Mr. Bergsma: "Look. I've managed a bar. I've had to fire people. I never do that without giving people a chance. What I say to people is, I didn't fire you, you fired yourself."

So that was *that* deal.

Benny cracked another beer while Gil made friendly Iowan noises to endorse the mild humor of the story.

Mr. Bergsma had hired all *kinds* of people—lawyers, agents, accountants, assistants, you *name* it—and they kept willfully firing themselves. To the point where he would explain the value of a fixer-upper in Pittsburgh from the get-go. You can get a house for as little as ten grand, he would explain. The *value* of it, obviously, is not simply the monetary value of whatever would otherwise have had to be paid for, the value is the amount of crap Mr. Bergsma's mind would otherwise have had to be clogged up with at a time when he might otherwise have been writing a fucking book.

Somehow, though, instead of picking up the ball and running with it, people began pre-firing themselves. To the point where Mr. Bergsma just had to do everything *himself.*

Benny went on, for illustrative purposes, for another 15 deals, winding up 10 hours and 30 beers later, at eight a.m. Eastern time (seven a.m. Central), not because more, much more could not be said, but because his audience was semi-comatose. What it all *explained* was why Benny was forced to sublet space in his loft.

"Not that I'm not glad to have you, dude," said Benny. "It's just the principle of the thing."

"Dude," said Gil, "I'm wrecked."

He sprawled on the bed beside the stranded backpack. Darkness claimed him.

With the wisdom of hindsight, it's interesting that Benny had this wealth of privileged information at his disposal for 27 *years*, while Gil, when he went into action, had had a mere smattering for little more than a week.

In the morning, or rather late afternoon, of Gil's second day in New York, he woke to find Benny incensed. A wall of the bathroom had this longstanding moldy seepage from the apartment upstairs. The seepage had now developed into a perceptible *flow*. It was the kind of thing Gil would have assumed was just *normal* in New York, but apparently a barrier had been crossed.

He would have liked to go back into Manhattan for pancakes, but an Iowan does not like to leave his fellow man in distress.

"Dude," he said, "hey, look, I'll go upstairs and see if I can fix whatever."

Gil's father had thought every boy should build his own tree-house; while not *typical* of Iowa, this is more easily achieved on a five-acre property with several 150-year-old trees than in a Manhattan apartment. Gil and his four brothers had each had a tree, and had, needless to say, engaged in cycles of competitive upgrading over the years, learning skills, as his father pointed out, that would stand them in good stead all their lives.[3] As now.

Gil had, obviously, brought his tool kit from home. He took it from the backpack and went upstairs and knocked on the door and a dude within told him to fuck off, which is so New York.

Gil talked on with the candid friendliness of the native Iowan. Presently (and he was too new in town to know how unthinkable this was) the dude opened the door a crack, leaving the chain on.

Gil talked nonjudgmentally on about the seepage escalation and his skills, such as they were, in plumbing and construction. The dude, eventually, did something even more unthinkable and let him in to see the source of the damage.

"Uh huh, uh huh," said Gil, looking at the standing pool around the base of the toilet. "Well, I'm pretty sure I can deal with this."

"We're going out of our minds is all," said the dude. "We're try-

---

3. If you have never thought of a treehouse as requiring plumbing and electricity, it's probably because you have never seen treehouse-construction as a competitive sport. You don't come from a family of boys, is the inference.

ing to do an IPO. We spend all our *time* interacting with people. We don't have interaction skills to spare, is the thing, on something like dealing with building management. And as for *plumbers, forget* it."

The dude was wearing a t-shirt that looked like an archaeological dig showing strata of pizza over the eons.

"See, if you decide that a user-friendly program needs an interactive paper clip to befriend a certain type of user," he said, "it's ultimately not a problem, because even if it does take more memory it's just a question of getting more RAM, we're talking a hundred bucks, max. But if you're doing software development you can't just upgrade the memory or processing speed of the human brain. *Yet.* To introduce spare capacity for dealing with morons. So there's trade-offs. So, obviously, we thought the IPO would be a done deal a year ago, but see, if we had diverted interaction capability to dealing with *plumbers* we would probably have alienated investors even *more.*"

Gil was nodding and opening up his tool kit and turning off the water supply. The dude remembered the importance of names for human interaction and provided his, which was Dave. He outlined the initial business plan and the unexpected obstacles it had encountered.

The initial business plan had been, if we get lots of money we can free up our own time to do inconceivably brilliant things and we can also hire some other really smart people and just free *them* up to do inconceivably brilliant things, and we can also hire lots of people who are not *that* smart and pay them to do all the boring things we don't want to do, freeing up even *more* of our own time for really interesting stuff. If we have enough people, we can deliver whatever we decide to do really fast[4] and it will make humon-

---

4. Dave and his partners had unhappily failed to read Frederick P. Brooks' *The Mythical Man-Month*. If this business plan sounds remotely plausible to you, you may want to read F. P. Brooks' classic work before proceeding.

gous amounts of money for people who are interested in money.[5]

This was a business plan that had worked for Dave's older brother in 1996, but in the climate of 2007 it had needed fleshing out. Dave had drawn the short straw and been forced to make presentations, and in the midst of a presentation he had commented that actually they were now thinking it might make more sense to just rebuild from scratch using Lisp.

Bad move.

It had then been necessary to make a lot more presentations to *new* investors, investors who had not heard about the Lisp idea and could still be shielded from the full brilliance of the dudes. Dave had been forced to buy a suit and wear the fucker. But by this time, though Dave had made the ultimate sacrifice, it was 2008, and in the climate of 2008 the amount of aggro involved was making them wonder whether *anything* could be worth that amount of aggro.

"Uh huh uh huh uh huh," said Gil, "do you have some kind of bucket or something I could use for the sources of blockage?"

"Um. A bucket?" said Dave. "Well, we maybe have some Colonel Sanders Chicken Buckets around, any good?"

"Good to go," said Gil. A small horde of roaches poured from the pipe like the wolf on the fold, their cohorts gleaming in basic roach black. All very New York, but Dave seemed unhappy with the development.

"Hey," said Gil. "I really need to replace this gasket anyway. I can pick up some roach stuff at the same time, no problem."

Not because Gil was exceptionally nice or helpful or friendly, by Iowan standards, but because this was the way *everyone* talked

---

5. Dave was, obviously, not explaining the details of the actual project to Gil, because explaining the project to clueless morons who know *nothing whatsoever* about programming was what he did, these days, for a living. No way was he going to squander what few vestiges of patience remained on a mere randomly presented plumber. We're talking nonrenewable resource here.

where he came from. It would not have won him any Brownie points back home, but Dave was charmed, disarmed.

Gil went back into Manhattan for a late late breakfast of pancakes. Harvey Keitel wasn't there today, but the point is, Gil was having pancakes knowing that *at any moment* Harvey Keitel might walk *in*. In some ways this was actually better than having Mr. Keitel physically on the premises. The pancakes were not, truth be told, better than his Mom's, but his Mom, obviously, could not offer the possibility of Harvey Keitel just walking in off the street.

He bought roach stuff and a gasket at a hardware store that had probably been there since 1847. He bought a bucket, dry plaster, and a trowel. He bought an item of signage indicating that sanitary products should be disposed of in the receptacle provided, and a receptacle.

La dolce vita was on at the Angelika!!!!!!!!!!!!!!

He had some time to kill, and while killing time he passed a bookstore, just walking down the street, and in the window was a collection of essays by John Cage!!!!!!!!!!!!!!! Which in future he could read over his pancakes in a place where, at any moment, Harvey Keitel might walk in.

After the film he got to talking to some dudes in the lobby, who invited him back to a party in their loft on Canal Street. In no time at all he was doing lines of cocaine with three investment bankers!!!!!!! Which was *exactly* why it was worth waiting to see *La dolce vita* in New York. At the age of 12 Gil had decided not to experiment with drugs, he wanted his first cocaine to be *special*, he wanted to try cocaine for the first time in New *York*, and it was definitely worth the wait. Because now, see, it was part of this whole *experience* of dressing like Bret Easton Ellis,[6] seeing *La*

---

6. Gil was wearing a slate gray shirt and slatier gray jacket that he had bought on eBay as looking like an ensemble seen in an author photo of Bret

dolce vita for the first time and going back to a loft to get high with three dudes from Morgan Stanley.

Gil started talking to a girl called Loopy Margaux, who said her dad had left his old job and gone to work for a hedge fund because it was less stressful.

"What was his *old* job?" asked Gil.

"Oh, arbitrage," said Loopy. "What's in the bag?"

Gil explained about the dudes upstairs and about the treehouse and such. With coke-fueled eloquence he elaborated on the sound system he had installed in his treehouse.

"*Oh*," said Loopy. "You know how to install *sound* systems? I should *introduce* you to my dad. He had one installed by someone all his friends use, and it's driving him *crazy*. If he took the business elsewhere word would get out and he would be *ostracized*. But if one of my *friends* came over it would be okay. Not that he wouldn't pay you for fixing it on a friendly basis."

"Sure," said Gil, "no problem," and meanwhile word percolated out that this was a man who had plumbing skills, electrical skills, construction skills and extermination skills, with none of the correlated obduracy, and in no time at all he had been offered three months' free accommodation in a loft in TriBeCa in return for fixing stuff its owner was temporarily unable to pay to get fixed. Plus the offer of two tickets to *Lohengrin* in return for fixing more minor stuff another dude was temporarily unable to pay to get fixed. Plus other prepaid entertainment opportunities too numerous to mention. Such that Gil was able to ask Loopy if she would like to see *Lohengrin* in two days' time and she said Yes!

It was nine a.m. Pancake time!

At two p.m., after a brief foray to the Metropolitan Museum

Easton Ellis, when in New York dress like Bret Easton Ellis being the thought; he attributed his ease in blending in, among real New Yorkers, to the infallible dress sense of Mr. Ellis.

of Art, he was back in Dumbo, back in his work jeans and a clean t-shirt, conferring upstairs with a different dude.

Dude B (Steve) said the dudes were thinking at this point they might be actually better off if they just went open *source*. If they went open source they would be dealing exclusively with their fellow hackers, and it would be *fun*.

"Uh huh uh huh," said Gil, laying out the wherewithal of roach death.

There was friction among the dudes, because Steve was a Perl guru, whereas Dave was a total Pythonista (not that Dave could not grok Perl or Steve Python, it was the philosophical *issues* under*lying* white space), but at least it was a relationship of mutual respect.[7] Where*as*.

Recently Dave had presented the software, which had some powerful mojo under the hood, to investors. The user interface had yet to be finalized, it was just this black-and-white thing. But all the investors could talk about was the UI.

"Uh huh uh huh," said Gil. "Yeah, funny, UI can totally eat up your time." He tightened the gasket. "Hey, if you do another presentation maybe you could do a Gantt chart using my Gantt chart app."

He began sweeping up roach remains.

"See, when I was a kid I had this Entenmann's cookie empire, where in the early days I would buy a box of Entenmann's for $1.19 and sell individual cookies for 25 cents at lunch and recess, and I kept growing my business to the point where I needed a web presence, and I had all these other irons in the fire, plus schoolwork. So I started doing Gantt charts in Excel. Which totally sucked, but I got a kick out of the Gantt charts, so I did an app, and yeah, it's amazing how much time it took doing the UI."

The dudes checked out Gil's Gantt chart app online and took in

---

7. Dude C, Gary, was the dude who had wanted to go back to first principles and use Lisp.

the cool UI. They checked out Gil's website, and the Mint analytics, similarly cool. A single brilliant idea occurred to the triumvirate.

Look. As things stand, using Dave for presentations, they are losing a minimum of one-third of their brainpower to fundraising crap. Instead of having three geniuses at work on the actual development they have two, and the work of those two is being delayed, in many cases, because they do not have stuff that Dave should have been developing.

But *look*. Why can't they just coopt not just the Gantt charts and the cool UI, but the creator of same? Why can't they just make Gil a partner and have him do the presentations? The company has, at a stroke, 100% of its genius power available for serious work! It means assigning maybe 15% of the stock options to Gil, but the massive gains in productivity will add such colossal value to the end product that they will, in the long term, end up getting *more*. In the short term they will not have to pay him a salary.

This cool idea was also, needless to say, a hand-me-down from Dave's older brother.

One with, you might think, little to recommend it at the worst time in history for an internet flotation.

Little to recommend it, at least, to a man with solid treehouse customization skills.

Gil, though, as it happened, had spent his teens fine-tuning his business plan, first just using Excel, then enhancing with a dashboard constructed in MicroCharts,[8] and he had also spent

---

8. MicroCharts is a plug-in for Excel which enables the user to replicate the sparklines of infoviz guru Edward Tufte, emeritus professor of graphic design, politics and economics at Yale. ET's pioneering *Visual Display of Quantitative Information* and its successors have never been reviewed in the *Wall Street Journal*, the *Financial Times* or the *Economist*; a sparkline, assuming you innocently placed your trust in the *WSJ*, *FT* or *Economist* to keep you au fait, is a small information-dense word-shaped graphic, enabling you to embed, as it might be, a time series or bar chart in text. MicroCharts, like its rival,

countless happy hours playing around with R, an open source statistical graphics package. *Then*, as a senior at the University of Iowa,[9] he had picked up a free academic license for Inference for R, a plug-in for Word and Excel which enables the user to insert R code and graphics directly into Word, or, as it might be, Excel. You set up your dataframe in R, you attach it to your document in Word or Excel, and hey presto! You can generate multivariate plots using Deepayan Sarkar's Lattice package! Directly in Word! Or, as it might be, Excel![10] Only problem was, it did not work in PowerPoint, which is, obviously, *the* weapon of choice for presentations. *But*, just before leaving home Gil had gotten an e-letter announcing an upgrade, such that Inference could now be used with PowerPoint.[11] Too late for his Entenmann's empire.

SparkMaker from Bissantz, runs only in Windows; Gil was a total Machead at heart, so he totally resented having to buy a whole separate laptop on eBay with Windows XP, after spending *hours* trying, to no avail, to get the fucker to work in Parallels or CrossOver or Boot Camp.

9. The appeal of the University of Iowa to an Iowan father of five is pretty much self-explanatory.

10. While R could be run in a Mac environment, Inference worked only in Windows, meaning that Gil spent further countless hours trying to get the fucker to work in Parallels or CrossOver or Boot Camp, finally retreating, bloody but unbowed, to his trusty Sony Vaio.

11. Having read ET's "The Cognitive Style of PowerPoint," Gil knew that his god saw PowerPoint as the work of the devil, so he did not feel good about wanting to use it. The Columbia Accident Investigation Board had concluded: "As information gets passed up an organizational hierarchy, from people who do analysis to mid-level managers to high-level leadership, key explanations and supporting information are filtered out ... it is easy to understand how a senior manager might read this PowerPoint slide and not realize that it addresses a life-threatening situation." *Hard* to feel good about colluding. But

Now, anyway, here was a chance to actually try out Inference in PowerPoint, with Lattice plots, in a legitimate business activity! And it was only his third day in New York!

On his fourth day in New York Gil went to B&H just to check the place out, because a tech store, run by Hasidic Jews, recommended by *Joel Spolsky* on joelonsoftware.com, it's hard to get more quintessentially New York than *that*. He talked to some dudes who were studying film at NYU and had just won a prize for a short at Sundance. He went to fourteen galleries on 11th Street, four of which were having vernissages that very night. He met a transvestite who had unresolved plumbing issues. He met a woman who had nearly been electrocuted by her refrigerator and said it was preying on her mind—who knew when it would lash out again?

On his fifth day in New York Gil went to see *Lohengrin* at the Met with Loopy Margaux. On his sixth day he met Mr. Margaux, who said his sound system had a mind of its own, with an IQ of about 68.

"Uh huh, uh huh," said Gil. There seemed to be no tactful way to say that he had better speakers in his treehouse. (His treehouse, admittedly, did not have a triptych by Francis Bacon, a Rauschenberg, a Jackson Pollock, and four flags by Jasper Johns.) He confined himself to the factual, making a number of recommendations which could easily be implemented with modest expenditure at B&H. He mentioned, shyly, the thing uppermost in his mind, the amazing Inference in Powerpoint presentation on which he had been

---

if you are addressing the business community people *expect* a PowerPoint presentation. *But*, if you could do a PowerPoint presentation drawing on the Trellis plots of Bill Cleveland of Bell Labs (from which the Lattice package derives), the presentation *would* be data-rich and it would be totally okay.

working for the past four days, and Mr. Margaux, as a personal favor, looked at the prez on Gil's laptop, and was sufficiently charmed to offer, as a further personal favor, to pass the word along to a couple of people who might be interested.

Gil walked back down the island through Central Park. He bought a New York hot dog with New York mustard and a New York pretzel. A troop of men on fixed-wheel bikes sped past. Pedestrians told them to fuck off. New York, New York, it's a wonderful town!

On his seventh day in New York Loopy Margaux had scary news. She had decided to move to Berlin.

"Ber*lin*?" said Gil.

Loops was 26 years old and had nothing to show for it. She was throwing her *life* away to keep a roof over her *shoe* collection. This was the gist.

"*Look*," said Loopy, and she took a print-out from her Marc Jacobs bag. "I can get a 1,000-square-foot apartment with 13-foot ceilings and crown molding for $800 a *month* including *bills*. *What* have I been *thinking*?"

If Loopy had explained that she had just tried cannibalism, and that human flesh actually tasted better than pork, this he could have coped with, because cannibalism, this is something that you can imagine a New Yorker, not any New Yorker but *some* kind of New Yorker, doing. Or if she had confessed to a string of serial killings. But moving to *Berlin*? And the whole shoe stockpiling thing, the point is, this is a very New York thing to do. The idea that you would rather have a month's rent in Berlin than a pair of Manolo Blahniks, well, huh.

Loops was saying she had sacrificed her goals, her dreams, everything she ever wanted to achieve, just to live in the City.

This sounded totally reasonable to Gil, who did not really care whether he ended up being a bartender, waiter, short-order cook, or homeless dude living out of a shopping cart as long as he could stay in New York,[12] but Loops made it sound like some kind of indictment.

Gil went back to the loft in Dumbo. *Brooklyn* was already starting to feel like exile. At some point he was going to have to break the bad news to Benny, namely that another dude must be found who had not read the *Automatika* series as a kid.

When he got in there was no sign of Benny. Instead there was a man who had the tormented, windswept look of Andrew Jackson as seen on a $20 bill.

"You must be Gil," said the dude. "I'm Benny's father. I had to come into town on business."

Gil had heard so much about Mr. Bergsma (one night had not been nearly enough to exhaust Benny's fund of aggrieved reminiscence) that he was surprised by how reasonable the dude sounded. Not a flamethrower in sight.

Gil said something polite. He wanted to try something new for his PowerPoint presentation. What if he used Hadley Wickham's ggplot2 package? He took out the Sony Vaio and was soon deep in thought.

Mr. Bergsma came up behind him.

"What's that?"

Gil explained the MicroCharts backstory, he explained about R and Bill Cleveland and Deepayan Sarkar and Hadley Wickham, and as he explained he did, in fact, generate a plot in Inference for R using ggplot2.

"When I was a kid my parents wouldn't even let me touch their Smith Corona," said Mr. Bergsma.

---

12. Did Giuliani realize that being President would involve moving to *Washington*? For four *years*? was the question Gil had naturally asked himself when the nomination was up for grabs. *Or,* was it just part of a deep-laid plan to move the nation's capital back to *New York,* where it *belonged*?

Gil remembered his chagrin at the belated release of Inference for R with PowerPoint interface. He could totally empathize.

"But yes, yes, yes, there is definitely a certain appeal. If they ever make the movie this kind of thing would be perfect for the *Automatika* machine."

"Is there going to be a movie?" asked Gil.

"All I want is a crap-free deal," said Mr. Bergsma. "It doesn't seem much to ask. What is there about the concept that is hard to grasp? I've been sent a contract which includes clauses about the ice show and theme restaurant rights. They want me to get it notarized. I can't just snap my fingers and conjure a notary public out of thin air."

He extended a longfingered, largeknuckled hand and gently stroked the glossy metal. "Sparklines, though. Multivariate plots. I was trying to think of something fun for the new *Automatika* book. This looks like something kids would get a kick out of. I'll just download this now, if you don't mind. Maybe I can do some actual *work* for a change." He sighed again. "Is it just me, or is there something sinister about Vista? Have you ever wondered whether the Church of Scientology might be behind it? It would explain so much."

Gil went back to tinkering with ggplot2.

When he looked up five hours later Mr. Bergsma was at the far end of the loft, typing morosely into an antiquated IBM ThinkPad.

Gil went out to the kitchen for a cold Sam Adams. The contract was in the trash. He took it out.

He started looking through the clauses, and for sure the contract went on a long time.

On Day 8 Gil went back to the Margaux' to finalize work on the sound system.[13] This time he met Mrs. Margaux, who turned out

---

13. He was not able to go back on Day 7, which was Saturday, because B&H is closed on Shabbat.

to be the woman with electrocution issues. Which he was naturally also only too happy to resolve.

"Uh huh, uh huh," said Gil, inspecting the rogue appliance, while Mrs. Margaux deplored Loopy's new plan.

"What if she comes back with a German boy?" said Mrs. Margaux. "I don't want to think of Hitler every time I sit down to dinner."

"Eeeeeezy does it," said Gil, edging the fridge gently forward.

"As if I don't have enough on my mind. Kooky Fairweather has *maneuvered* me into resigning from the Board of the Met. Lottie Rosenthal has just asked Dodie *Pierpont* onto the Board of the Balanchine. I can't take much more of this."

"Uh huh, uh huh," said Gil. "Yep, I think I see what the problem is." Three tiny mice slept unsuspectingly in a small nest of shredded paper towel.

Mrs. Margaux explained that *meanwhile*, in just the last *month*, eight of her *closest personal friends* had been coopted onto the boards of eight grant-making foundations for the arts, and she had not even been *asked*.

"Mmmm," said Gil. He dropped a chamois on top of the nest and swept it nonchalantly up and into his tool kit. Though extermination, probably, awaited the rest of the family. "*Well*, what you *could* do ..."

"Yes?" said Mrs. Margaux. (What could a mere Iowan know of the cutthroat world of New York philanthropy?)

"... is outflank. I don't know if you know this, but J. P. Bergsma has this thing about wanting a fixer-upper in Pittsburgh."

"*Pittsburgh*?" said Mrs. Margaux.

"I know," said Gil. "I *know*. But see."

He was about to make a simple, crap-free suggestion, to the effect that Mrs. M could end the 13-year dry spell of this much-loved author and be instrumental in facilitating a much-longed-for film, simply by organizing the unpopular Pittsburgh fixer-upper element which had been a stumbling block so many times in the past.

One of his 200 newfound friends was a dude whose brother was a subcontractor in Pittsburgh, a dude facing problems because the developer he was working for had suddenly filed for bankruptcy. How hard could it be?

Fixing things on a case-by-case basis, though, is such an inelegant solution. It lacks scalability. It lacks grandeur. And it doesn't give you *data*, that you can *analyze*. Where*as*.

He said, "See, for ten, fifteen, twenty-thousand dollars you can get a house. A residency is normally for a maximum of 8 weeks. A typical grant is for $45,000, $50,000 for a year. *So*, say you go to these 8 entities, you offer the grant of a fixer-upper, for the people on the shortlist who didn't make the grade. Among whom Mr. Bergsma is merely one. In return for a percentage of whatever artistic earnings they achieve over, say, 10 years. With some kind of cap? Making it, potentially, self-sustainable? Do a different city every year? Allow swaps? You then *compare* the achievements of your also-rans with those who got the actual *award*. And see, you could have a web presence, you could have something like minglebee's MotoGP dataviz, that lets you *drill down* to look at individual performance? And Mr. Margaux could potentially even devise an investment vehicle?"

The refrigerator was purring softly. Mrs. Margaux was initially skeptical, but when Gil called up www.minglebee.com, and she was able to see for herself the fun that could be had drilling down, *well*. Adam got so cross when people kept asking him for checks, but my goodness, this would actually be *fun*. Gil left her clicking on drivers in the Malaysian Motorcycle Grand Prix, 10/19/2008.

This elegant solution had the drawback of deferring, probably indefinitely, the resolution of Mr. Bergsma's specific problem. Mr. Bergsma was saved, in this instance, by circumstances beyond his control.

The dudes who had won at Sundance, who thought funding was solid for their first feature, had suddenly found that the money had dried up because the producers wanted something guaranteed bankable and commercial. But the dudes had a soft spot for *Automatika*, the one commercial project they could even *contemplate*, unsurprisingly, really, because the kind of dude you would meet in B&H is the kind of dude who would have been that kind of kid as a kid. *And*, another of Gil's 200 newfound friends was an entertainment lawyer with extermination issues. *So*, though it was not really in the spirit of rigorous experiment design, Gil pushed ahead.

Within a day it was the donest of deals. The lawyer's extermination issues had been resolved; a crap-free two-pager, with an unconventional real estate clause, had been sent to Gil as a PDF attachment. The subcontractor had agreed to organize purchase and fixing-up of a fixer-upper in Pittsburgh, within walking distance of Carnegie Mellon, subject to bank appeasement. One of the NYU dudes had lowered himself to make contact with his contact at Fox. Fox wanted in. And Mr. Bergsma, presented with the deal, had assigned the rights, minus the costs of the Pittsburgh fixer-upper, to Benny.

Mrs. Margaux, meanwhile, brought pressure to bear on Mr. Margaux; within a week she was able to go to her "friends" with an offer they could not, in all decency, refuse, using the new vocabulary item "drilling down" to killing effect.

Time passes.

The Dumbo dudes achieve a successful flotation and do, in fact, do something so inconceivably brilliant that their investors are happier than they could reasonably have expected. Thanks to the Iowan Investor Interface the dudes are spared actual personal contact with said investors, so they too are happier than they could reasonably have expected.

Mr. Bergsma moves to Pittsburgh and immerses himself in his *Automatika* world. Fifty creative types move to Pittsburgh and comprehensively outperform the types who pipped them to the post in their initial grant applications. The subcontractor realigns his construction business. *Automatika* the movie succeeds beyond the wildest dreams of the NYU dudes, such that they can select their projects. Loopy Margaux packs the bare essentials (five suitcases of shoes) and goes to Berlin to pursue her dream. Mr. Margaux has fun. While the actual money involved is peanuts, his genius for applying financial acumen to support of the arts *and* urban renewal is noticed at the White House. Mrs. Margaux is the envy of her friends.

Benny gets $500,000.

Benny got what he always said he wanted, the freedom to do what he wanted. He's not as happy as he might have expected.

Mr. Bergsma had been talking for *years* about the kind of deal he was looking for, and Benny, Lord knows, had the inside track. So what was to stop *Benny* from pulling a CFD out of a hat? What was to stop *Benny* from finagling the fixer-upper? What was to stop *Benny* from expanding the Pittsburgh idea, to the point where Mr. Bergsma looked like a visionary instead of a crank? Meanwhile some kid just walks in the door, a kid who has never even read the *books*, and hands him the CFD on a plate. The son he never had.

Benny hates talking to people about his father.

Gil, needless to say, moves into Manhattan, where he lives to this day.

Remember Me

Gerald was only a Canon in the Cathedral, not a very forceful one. He put it to the Bishop that it might be A Good Thing to invite a Jew to participate in the VE-Day service, and the Bishop waved a hand affably, as who should say, if a Jew can be *found* it might not be a bad thing at *all*. Gerald made noises to the local Rabbi, who could not personally undertake but put him on to a man who might do.

Gerald got on to the man. He had not had much to do with Jews, but the fellow seemed pleasant enough.

Gerald mooted. The fellow began to talk excitedly, throwing out all sorts of wild ideas which seemed to involve *rather* a lot of *Hebrew*. Gerald could not *quite* see where all this was to be slotted into the service, *nor*, come to that, what the *Bishop* would make of it all. He explained diffidently that he had really rather thought that perhaps the fellow might be willing to read the Old Testament reading for the day.

'*Oh*, I *see*,' said the fellow. 'You'd like a *Jew* to read from the *Old Testament*.'

'Er, yes,' said Gerald.

'I'm not interested, thanks,' said the fellow. Hung up the phone.

The Bishop's withers were thankfully unwrung.

K had seen too much of this sort of thing to be disenchanted.

He sang lustily:

Thus, on the fateful banks of Nile
Weeps the deceitful crrrrrocodile!
Thus hypocrites that murder act
Make Heav'n and Gods the author of the fact!

—By all that's good
—No more!
All that's good you have foreswore
To your prrrrromised Empire fly
And let forsaken—Dido—die!

Ha ha!

(K had Purcell very much on his mind, though his thoughts had been running chiefly in the direction of *The Fairy Queen*; he was to be married in the fall. He had a pronounced aversion to the Wedding March from *Lohengrin* as nuptial accompaniment.)

The regular association of ideas naturally led K at this point to walk down to Blockbuster to borrow the DVD of *Kiss Me Deadly*. Only to find—*O tempora, o mores!*—that his trusty Blockbuster was no more. (It had been one of the *good* ones.) Enquiries at his hotel elicited the suggestion that he watch the thing on his laptop by streaming it off Amazon. Pfui!

Gerald discovered, somewhat late in the day, that this would have been the most terrific *coup*. He had once read a novel by Iris Murdoch and had not enjoyed it; for the most part the word 'contemporary' sufficed to put him off a work of fiction. He had never heard of K. He happened to mention the incident in a moment of fretfulness to one of the younger Canons and was told that K was in the running for a Nobel Prize. Oh my ears and whiskers! The man's name, mercifully, had never happened to come up in water-testings with the Bishop.

•

K had gone back to England for a few months to do research and organise documentation for his wedding.

K, as he had often expatiated, had nothing against marriage provided it was sufficiently ritualised. It seemed a modest requirement, but when he did in fact engage to marry people kept trying to clutter up the ritual with effusions of sincerity. K simply wanted the Hebrew text in the programme and if people wanted to feel something that was entirely their own affair. (K's views on the *Kaddish* of Mr Leon Wieseltier, in which the Aramaic text is conspicuous by its absence, may readily be imagined.) He had thought that in New York, of all places, this would be simple enough to arrange, but as it turned out none of the printers they approached had anything remotely suitable. He was left to try to drum up something passable in Golders Green. A strategic sortie to Glyndebourne, where they were putting on a delectable *Rosenkavalier*, palliated the anguish. (Printers! Gaaaa!)

K returned to New York at the end of the summer and was chagrined to discover that *Der Freischütz* was on at the Met on Erev Yom Kippur. Damn and Blast! He worked out that he could snatch a last meal, just, before the curtain went up and begin his fast during the first act.

An excellent plan in its way, it meant that he was hors de combat when social arrangements were made during a longueur in Kol Nidrei. K's fiancée, Rachael, invited a friend to join them in breaking their fast.

(Thanks to the mixed seating so popular in America, K could easily have put the kaboosh on the plan had he not succumbed to the superior charms of *Der Freischütz*.)

The meal could be said to have had its uses. There's something to be said for allowing a fiancée to learn, *early in the relationship,* the sort of occasion one goes out of one's way to avoid.

•

The friend, Eloise, had started life as a Presbyterian. She had converted in England; she had undergone ritual immersion at Henley, where it had been necessary to dodge rowers warming up for the regatta. She had in fact broken up with the boyfriend for whose sake, or rather, for whose mother's sake, the conversion had been embarked upon, but Simon had said it would be rude to the rabbi to drop out. Permission to work in the UK, which would have accompanied marriage to Simon, was now out of reach, so she had returned without enthusiasm to New York. She had attended services on Yom Kippur because it seemed obscurely rude to the rabbi not to bother. It had seemed obscurely rude to the rabbi to skimp. Hence Kol Nidrei. (All this, naturally, part of what passed for conversation at dinner.)

The girl's Hebrew was not at all good. (Her personal best for the Amidah was a shamemaking 25 minutes.) With the result, unsurprisingly, that she had whiled away the forcefasted hours reading the English pages facing the impenetrable Hebrew of her shabby Machzor.

720 pages into Birnbaum the child had come upon Isaiah 57:14–58:14. (Quotation from which cannot help but seem long to the sort of person for whom an hour is a reasonable length for a service. What is to be done? Pah!)

There is no peace for the wicked, says my God.
Cry out, spare not, raise your voice like a trumpet;
Tell my people their guilt, tell Jacob's house their sins,
Daily indeed they seek me, desiring to know my ways;
As an upright nation that has not forsaken the laws of its God,
They keep asking me about righteous ordinances;

[footnote from Birnbaum: ולס ולס, the prophetic portion recited as the *haftarah*, refers to the fasts. The people have complained that their fasts have produced no change in their material welfare. The prophet replies that their fasting was a hollow pretence. [!!!] Instead of giving their workmen a holiday, they worked them all the harder. If they would but feed the hungry and nurture the destitute, God would lift them out of their miserable conditions. [!!!!!!!!]]

They seemingly delight to draw near to God.
'Why seest thou not,' they ask, 'when we fast?'
'Why heedest thou not when we afflict ourselves?'
Behold, on your fast day you find business,
And you drive on all who toil for you.
Your fasting is amidst contention and strife,
While you are striking with a godless fist;
You do not fast today to make your voice heard on high.

Can such be my chosen fast, the day of man's self-denial?
    [!!!!!]
To bow down his head like a bulrush, to sit in sackcloth and
    ashes?
Is that what you call fasting, a day acceptable to the Lord?
Behold, this is the fast that I esteem precious:
Loosen the chains of wickedness, undo the bonds of oppres-
    sion,
Let the crushed go free, break all yokes of tyranny!
Share your food with the hungry, take the poor to your
    home, [!!!!!!!]
Clothe the naked when you see them, never turn from your
    fellow,

Then shall your light dawn, your healing shall come soon;
Your triumph shall go before you, the Lord's glory backing
you.

[footnote from Birnbaum: … פתח חרצבו that is, God favors
the fast that includes ת the self-denial shown in the exercise
of justice and kindness; for example, setting the people free
and distributing food and clothing. [!!!!!]]

The synagogue was very full, for it was a day of competitive fasting.
The girl thought: But perhaps at this very moment there are Jews
manning soup kitchens, having taken this passage of Isaiah to heart
… So they would naturally not be in synagogue. Perhaps the sort of
person who goes to synagogue fasting is not the sort of person who
would take Isaiah to heart. So perhaps it was not odd that EVERY-
ONE did not stand up and walk out and give a homeless person a
place to stay. But was it not odd that *not one person* did so? (This too,
naturally, part of what passed for conversation at dinner.)

Ah, said K, but you're taking it out of context. The interpretation of the text is determined by the oral tradition. You can't
cherrypick. If you're going to reject the oral tradition, it's not clear
what you're doing there in the first place. Why are you willing to
accord special status to this text on the basis of its presence on an
occasion whose importance is determined by tradition?

It would have been possible for Eloise to say something about
Agamben at this point, but she felt awkward, now, meeting K.

K was an Abstract Situationist. His sentences had their cold
beauty.

He stated in interviews that art should concern itself with the
operation of the machine.

The operation of the social machinery, he would add for clar-
ity, though he disliked the phrase.

K was very grand, so grand that he could refer to himself as K in his work without a murmur of editorial dissent. Eloise was very young and not at all grand. She had known K's work for years and had imagined that it was open to anyone to follow his example, or rather that it was open not only to K but to anyone to follow the example of the usual suspects. If K had this licence only in virtue of his position he would, as an avowed Situationist, have embedded a statement to this effect in the work—so she had thought, being a mere Naïve Situationist at the time.

She had been wrong about this as about so many other things.

Eloise had written a book and been made to have discussions in which the phrase 'flesh out' was used of characters. She was just out of college. She had been reading Robbe-Grillet. She had recently seen *Dogville*. In a moment of weakness she had attached to four characters the sort of name that is affixed to a little primate at birth. Each was also provided with hair, eye, and skin colour, a wardrobe, some sort of plausible history. A favourite TV show. What with all these plausible names and histories, the characters went plausibly about their business like impostors in a witness protection programme. It was, of course, awkward to be known to K as the person whose name appeared on the cover of the thing.

(She was, as it happened, safe enough: the word 'contemporary' was enough to put K off a work of fiction.)

K, meanwhile, talked on.

K drew attention to the difference between a cliché and a formula. (He preferred the fixed formulae of the Homeric poems to the polished phrases of Vergil.) K had once read an essay by Harold Bloom in which the great man found fault with J. K. Rowling for using the phrase 'he stretched his legs' whenever a character went for a walk. K had immediately lost all respect for Harold Bloom, who appeared not only to be unfamiliar with Milman Parry's *The Making of Homeric Verse* but also to be wholly innocent of the *Iliad*, *Odyssey*, *Homeric Hymns*, Epic Cycle and *Argonautica* except, perhaps, in some sort of translation. Taken to its logical conclusion, the argument would compel one to prefer the *Argonautica* to the *Iliad*. Madness! (K had tried to do a search in the Perseus project for ton d'apameibomenos prosephe (that old Homeric wordhorse), was balked by an uncooperative search engine, left Bloom with a shrug unenlightened.) The problem with J.K.R. was not that she was repetitive, nor even that she was not repetitive enough, but rather that she was insufficiently formulaic. Judging by the 3 pages K had been able to bring himself to read before remembering that we are creatures of a day.

All this time Eloise was working up her courage. K loved to say of the Greeks that they experienced their subjectivity as a trajectory through a nexus of social interstices, linguistic artifacts cast in or broken by the machinery of legal systems. To hear K discourse on the character of Odysseus in Sophocles' *Ajax* was to have a memory to save up for one's grandchildren. Surely K, then, would not be blind to the predicament of one required to engage with the modern machinery of the law?

Eloise's situation was that she had written a new book, one which required the legal muscle enjoyed by K if its characters were not to find themselves in a witness protection programme. K was so grand that his contracts were negotiated by someone very grand indeed. Eloise's lawyer, who was not at all grand, claimed that the boilerplate was non-negotiable. Eloise had the true hacker's love of economy of effort; K had a perfectly good contract negotiated by a master of the art, on which her unloved lawyer was unlikely to improve; why could this unimprovable document not be redeployed? When they were all very drunk (they had fasted, after all, for a night and a day) Eloise put this ingenious suggestion to K, who said he was not comfortable mixing business with friendship.

The formulaic reply made it clear that K was not new to ingenious suggestions.

•

K had more serious matters to contend with. He was in the midst of protracted negotiations of a delicate nature. The mother of his bride would not brook kosher catering for the wedding. His sister, who had joined the Lubavitch after a turbulent youth, would not permit her seven children to eat cake if it were not kosher. It would be cruel and inhumane to invite children to a party at which they could not eat cake; K's soft heart melted. The points at issue were whether, on the one hand, a kosher cake from an approved purveyor might pass muster with his sister, provided the cake were kept strictly segregated from all other comestibles, and whether, on the other hand, such cake might be acceptable to a non-religious fanatic.

> One charming Night
> Brings more delight
> Than a hundred, than a hundred, than a hundred lucky Days—

Eloise's editor left for another job. The new editor was unenthusiastic with the legacy. No contract had been signed. The characters were given an unexpected reprieve from the witness protection programme.

Eloise was introduced to an agent who sold her book in a week. The book had been in a mixture of first, second and third persons; the editor thought it would work much better if it were all in first.

K and his bride found an apartment on Central Park West, easy walking distance to Lincoln Center and a shul with an intelligent rabbi.

K published to acclaim a book which alternated between first, second and third persons.

•

K was not at all sporting about the thing with the Cathedral. He shared it genially with his friends at shul, mischievously at dinner parties. Americans naturally like to hear that the British are stuck in the mud; the story was passed round to the point where Nigel, an ambitious young Canon at Bath and Wells, heard it three times in a single day on a trip to New York.

Eloise's new editor left for another job. The replacement examined the legacy and saw at once that the book would work better in third person.

K won a prize for the new book, thus becoming much grander.

Nigel had been keeping his ear to the ground. He saw at once that the thing, used properly, might just do for his Bishop, who was quietly pining for a shot at Canterbury. It would be the most terrific *coup* if Bath and Wells could persuade the now indisputably distinguished K to accept *carte blanche.*

By the most extraordinary piece of luck, Boulez agreed to come to London to revive his production of *Moses und Aron.*

Nigel whispered in the ear of a very dear friend at Covent Garden: it would be *quite wonderful* if Boulez and K were to appear in conversation before the great event. Boulez was, in fact, an admirer of K; K agreed to the treat (with the promise of accommodation at Claridge's and a box for opening night).

Nigel was then able quite naturally to reply to K's benevolent thanks for his efforts.

The Bishop and Mrs Bishop trusted him implicitly; if an invitation to the Glyndebourne *Arabella* would lure the Nobel laureate in posse, to Glyndebourne they would go. Mrs Bishop handsomely undertook to lay on hampers from Fortnum's, strictly kosher in case of need—one could always count on Mrs B.

K was all amiability in agreeing to join the episcopal party. He was not, in fact, at all particular in matters of kashrut, but he very much liked to be asked.

At supper he displayed his broadmindedness by consuming lobster patties with evident enjoyment.

Nigel was assiduous in filling his glass with champagne.

At the second interval K agreed affably to contribute to a service apiece at Bath and at Wells. He knew printers at Golders Green who could sort out the Hebrew. Mrs B. (bless her) made all the right noises.

Gerald's Bishop remained thankfully unapprised.

Climbers

"The thing you have to understand is that I really don't understand people."

Gil sat on a squashy old sofa, legs akimbo, forearms on thighs. He was wearing a dark green polo shirt with a small red turtle in the place where a more fashionable polo shirt sports a crocodile. It had the trusting incomprehension of a Presidential dog.

"I mean for instance. Peter Dijkstra. There are these people, they totally say *Dude*, Peter *Dijkstra*, I *love* Peter Dijkstra, what a *genius*, but then they say, Oh, but he's *impossible*, we met him for drinks in Amsterdam and he spent the whole night talking to the bartender's *dog*! And then he walked off with Jason's *brand new Moleskine*!!!!"

It is not new information that he wore a dark green polo shirt with a turtle on the left breast, but sometimes we can't be rational. If a garment quietly clothes its owner while he speaks, this cannot be uncomplaining loyalty, it cannot be touching, because this is what garments do. (What *else* would it do? Walk off in a huff?) And yet there was a touching loyalty in the quiet uncomplaining persistence of the turtle on the dark green breast. It had been there and it was still there.

"But see, this is what I don't understand. Because see. Say Peter Dijkstra comes to New York and needs a place to stay, he can come to my place and stay as long as he wants and I'll just go off and couch surf with friends to get out of his way."

The friendly crowd let him talk uninterruptedly on. They filled the loft that would be placed so gladhandedly at the disposal of Peter Dijkstra.

"Okay, now let's say I'm off the premises and Peter Dijkstra rents a van and loads it up with everything I own. I go back and everything is gone. Books, CDs, DVDs, TV, computer, baseball cards. *Gone*. And it's not just the stuff, Peter Dijkstra went through my papers, my personal papers, and he took my diaries, and my notebooks, and my photo albums, all this incredibly personal, irreplaceable paraphernalia, he just took it. The place is empty. All I've got is the clothes I'm standing in, my laptop, and my iPhone. So I'm standing in this empty apartment, and I'm looking around, and the point is, I'm *happy*. I'm *ecstatic*. Peter Dijkstra—Peter Dijkstra!!!!—has appropriated this stuff, in some mysterious way my stuff is going to contribute to a book by Peter Dijkstra! I feel *honored*. I mean, the stuff is not contributing to a work of genius just sitting there in my apartment."

What could anyone do but smile and feel shamefaced, crass? It was as if he was the only one in the room unconscious of the reviews, the prizes, the sales. With a little luck someone might compete for the reviews, the prizes, the sales, but who could compete for the absence of consciousness?

(The unpretentiousness of the humble turtle—it's hard to explain how this contributed to making people feel shamefaced and crass, but it did.)

"So the thing of it is, is that Peter Dijkstra does not have it in his power to betray me, if he thinks something of mine can help with his new book he can just have it. Not only is he not letting me *down*, this has been a fantasy ever since I was a kid. I don't care about the things, it just makes me happy to be part of this. So when I say a writer is a genius, what I mean is, there is nothing I won't do for him. It's really simple. Same thing with friends. When I use the word 'friend' what I mean is, 'What's mine is yours.' It's really really really really simple."

People were laughing, smiling, drinking their beers. It was kind of upbeat to hear except that presumably, then, no one in the room was even a friend?

Rachel sat cross-legged at the other end of the squashy sofa. Silky black hair drifted over her shoulders; glass-green eyes, a bittersweet mouth endorsed uncalculating simplicity with their beauty. She wore a black t-shirt with white stick figures who said:

MAKE ME A SANDWICH
                    WHAT? MAKE IT YOURSELF
SUDO MAKE ME A SANDWICH
                    OKAY

This t-shirt too had the lovable cuteness of the First Dog.

Cissy stood at the back of the crowd in the cruel grip of consciousness.

Cissy had met Peter Dijkstra in Vienna. She had booked a room through venere.de but it had fallen through: an apologetic e-mail in exquisitely courteous German had explained that the room had gone through another booking service a few minutes earlier. She had been offered an alternative but instead had found Angel's Place through booking.com, closer to the center and with the look, somehow, of a hi-tech monastery. The rooms were underground, with very white plaster walls, arched ceilings of bare brick, and fierce gleaming black flat-screen TVs. It was enchanting. And then there were only four rooms, so unlike the free-for-all of a hostel, it would be silent, pure, a place to read and think and write. And so she had taken the train down from Prague and checked in late and gone out in the morning for Sachertorte at Oberlaa Kurkonditorei and wandered all day.

She got back very late, close to midnight. In the breakfast room at street level a man sat at a table reading. He held a pen; a notebook was open. It was as if she had walked into a hotel and found Wittgenstein writing quietly at a table.

He looked older, wearier than in the only picture anyone had seen, though his very pale hair would not show gray. He was unassumingly dressed in the way that older Europeans are unassuming: he wore a short-sleeved blue-and-white checked shirt, well, white with pale blue double lines in a grid, and faded gray pants, and stout brown walking shoes. He did not bother to look up when she came in.

She could not bring herself to speak. She could not bring herself to go to her room. She went to the kitchen for a glass of water. She heard the scrape of his chair. When she turned she saw him standing, holding a pack of Marlboros. He went to the door and into the street.

The book, she saw, was Detlev Claussen's biography of Adorno; he had left it open face down on the table. She would have liked to look at the writing on the page of the open notebook but she knew it would be bad. She put water into the coffee machine and slotted in a capsule of espresso.

The door opened just as the coffee began to drip into the little plain cup.

She knew she would hate herself always if she did not speak. She said, "You're Peter Dijkstra, aren't you? I love your work."

He said, "Thank you."

She said, "Do you like Vienna?"

He said, "Very much. It's my first time, for one reason and another." (She knew that he had been in an asylum for five years.)

He said, "They speak German like robots. It's pleasant hearing a language mechanically spoken. I wish I had known."

He said, "Adorno came as a young man to study with Alban Berg. Claussen is quite amusing on the subject."

But he had picked up the book and put his pen in the fold to mark his place and closed it and he was picking up his notebook.

"Don't let me disturb you," she said. "I was just going to bed."

"So am I," he said. "That was my last cigarette for the day."

In the morning she asked Angel if she could extend her booking for a week.

She would have liked to tell this story, she desperately wanted to tell this story and be drawn to the squashy sofa to be pumped for details, singled out for envious excited questions and exclamations and comments, enfolded in the collective embrace. But she had not been invited. Nathan had told her to come because Gil was a friendly guy, but he had not been able to introduce her while Gil was talking and now he was talking to other friends.

She stood awkwardly at the back.

Across the room she saw Ralph, who had found a publisher for her book when no one was buying. He caught her eye and smiled and she drifted across. He wore a pale aqua polo shirt with a crocodile on the breast, chinos, and sockless Topsiders, because he had never wanted to be a suit.

He had not done for her what he had done for Rachel, who floated now on a magic carpet.

"You should represent Peter Dijkstra!" she said gaily. "I met him in Vienna. I could put you in touch!" It felt like a thing to be doing. She imagined Peter Dijkstra in New York. There would be an inner circle of admirers. Some kind of dinner, maybe, conferring over what could be done for the genius. Sontag had introduced Sebald to New Directions.

Peter Dijkstra in New York, the inner circle, Sontag, Sebald, New Directions—she was not the only dreamer in the room.

Peter Dijkstra lay on a very white bed, his head on his arm. The television was on; German tripped off the metal tongue of a female chat show host.

At 2 am he went upstairs with his laptop and cigarettes.

An e-mail from his editor at Meulenhoff forwarded five e-mails from altruists across the pond, relaying the declared devotion of a young American writer of some fame.

He went outside to smoke a cigarette.

He did not want to be locked up again. He was sane enough as long as he lay on the bed watching TV, or stood in the street smoking a cigarette, but it's true, the bills did mount up. He was sheltering under his credit cards.

Somehow, though. The fact that a fame-kissed young American would happily hand over all his worldly goods did not make it socially straightforward to write asking for a gift of 20,000 euros. If something was not socially straightforward he could feel his mind cracking. He wondered whether the boy might in fact give him a place to stay if he went to New York but it seemed terribly complicated. If the boy did move out it would be all right, but if he did not it would be impossible. He could not think of any sentences that would ascertain the position in a socially acceptable fashion.

Anyway, it was comfortable among the robots. Americans are so natural and friendly and sincere. The Viennese have the mechanical predictable charm of a music box; you don't have to *warm* to it. He would have liked it if the boy had set up an account for him at a pastry shop. That would have been a nice gesture. The Wiener Phil—imagine if an admiring reader were to give him a subscription! Americans do like you to warm to them, and he thought he might very well warm to someone who gave him a subscription to the Wiener Phil, but it did not seem a very American thing to do. An American, he thought, would see it as too finely tuned.

A Hungarian might do something lavish and extravagant along those lines. He might keep madness further at bay if he took to writing in Hungarian.

Come to think of it, a limitless supply of Marlboros would not come amiss—but no, an American would find that quite shocking.

Cissy knew she had to be in New York, and she knew Ralph had to do the things he was doing for her, but oh! it was horrible, grubby and horrible. People he knew had read her book and sent quotable quotes and now her book would be plastered with names of people whose work she despised. Was it like this in Europe? She wished she was back in the white cellar with its brick walls and its green-and-white tiled bathroom and its gleaming black flat-screen TV. It would be so different, so different and good, if her book were read by a man in an unassuming check shirt who smoked Marlboros and called Adorno Teddie Wiesengrund the Wunderkind. It wasn't about the quotes, though if the name could go in the book with all the others plastered there she would not feel so sick.

She ran into Rachel at a party at the KGB. She said, "I think we should do something for Peter Dijkstra!" (She did not know if Ralph had asked Rachel, and this way she did not have to think about it.) She talked wildly and impulsively and enthusiastically.

Rachel said, "Well, I love Peter Dijkstra." She wore skinny white jeans and a sloppy lilac-blue v-necked sweater, sleeves rucked up to her elbows, cashmere. She was drinking Campari. She said, "But I don't know. He seems pretty private, or at least that's the way I imagine. Let's see what Gil has to say."

Gil had come back from the bar. He said, "I'm a sucker for really good vodka. They have stuff here you just don't see anywhere else. I'm behind on a deadline, but hey, maybe there's a *reason* for that. Maybe the piece *needed* an authentic Russian vodka with an authentically unpronounceable name."

Cissy told the story of walking into Angel's Place. She said it was like walking into a hotel and seeing Wittgenstein writing at a table.

"Awesome!" said Gil. He did not pump her for details, but she gave some anyway.

She said, "I think we should do something!"

"What kind of thing?" said Gil.

She did not really know. She did not know enough to know the kind of thing. She babbled about conferences, readings, a lecture. She said he should have a trade publisher, like Sebald, a book deal with a lot of money.

Gil took a swallow of vodka. "Ahhhh," he said.

"I don't know," he said. "I mean. The thing is, there are people who like that kind of thing. They like hustling, and they're good at it. But even so they don't just run out in the street and randomly hustle, they get approval, an arrangement, authorization. Those might be good things for him, but I wouldn't feel comfortable rushing around and *orchestrating* on his behalf. And the other thing is, I'd be afraid of losing something that really means a lot to me, something very precious. Something I *need* so much I can't imagine life without it. What if it changed the books for me? What if I no longer had them for myself in this private place where it's just me and the book? It doesn't work that way for people who like hustling, you don't get the impression that agents have lost something they loved. But maybe that's why it makes sense for that kind of person to do that kind of work. Does he have an agent? Maybe he should talk to Ralph."

"I did talk to Ralph about it, but he made regretful noises about the market for translations."

"Oh, Ralph says these things but he's just trying to be sensible because he's so impulsive." Rachel, indulgent. "If he falls in love with a book he'll *besiege* people."

Ralph was not an intellectual but maybe the secret of success was not caring. Or maybe an actual genius would be so far above, would be used to being so far above, that it wouldn't matter.

Maybe it would matter, though, that Ralph was so careful to be cautious. If you went to a café he would order wheatgrass juice and gluten-free toast with tapenade—that is, he would insist on going to the kind of café where you could order these things. Maybe a man who had spent five years in an asylum needed someone who stayed sane without effort.

Cissy knew it was not safe to say these things to Rachel. The magic carpet had carried her on but Ralph was still a good friend.

Needless to say, crowdsourcing a limitless supply of Marlboros was not an idea whose time had come.

Partly to keep madness at bay, and partly to take the most direct route to keeping his credit cards afloat, he was writing in English. He could not see the point of writing in Dutch in the hope that he would join the elect. Why should he get the lucky ticket and be translated and touted? He had had two novellas and some stories turned into English by the kind of publisher that will publish novellas and stories, and though the phrase "cult classic" had come to his ears it did not buy many Marlboros. This is what you get if you are dependent on an editor whose wife happens to know some Dutch. But if you write in English you can send the thing anywhere, you can send it to the big boys, people who wouldn't touch a novella with a bargepole.

He had a little pack of file cards on which he wrote words and phrases that took his fancy, and he constructed stories out of them. Stories, okay, not the fast track to debt-free nirvana, but you can't be always breathing down your own neck. Think of *Gurrelieder*. Something that starts out small and self-contained can morph ("morph"! English is so great!) into an extravaganza. You have to give the horse its bit.

He was sane enough to spot likely words in a text, and sane

enough to write them on a file card, and sane enough to string them together, or rather doing these things kept his mind quiet and good. He didn't know if he could do much more. But it was nice not having to be cheery and down-to-earth and sensible for cheery sensible down-to-earth Dutch nurses and orderlies. It was okay now to lie quietly on the bed staring at the wall.

He got an effusive e-mail from the girl who had made coffee late one night.

Probably she got his address from the people who published the novellas.

He wrote a polite reply.

An effusive reply came within 10 minutes. There was a lot more sincerity than he knew what to do with.

She mentioned talking to her agent and his regretful comments on translation in the United States.

He was already a bit tired but clearly this was a lead which must be followed. He explained a little about the file cards and writing in English.

Fifteen minutes later, when he was starting to hope that was an end of it, a new message popped up. She had talked to her agent who would love to see some pages.

He could not say why, but he really disliked that use of the word "pages."

At this point he was ready to go back to bed.

This was not the way to deal with all those credit cards.

She had included the agent's e-mail address. He clicked on it and attached a Word document (after all these years he still hated Word). He explained to the agent that he normally wrote in longhand but this was what he had happened to type up.

He went outside and lit a Marlboro. If he ever had a lot of

money, really a lot of money, he would just buy this place and then he could smoke inside.

Ralph called Cissy because he was simply besotted with the pages, he had devoured them at a single gulp, if the rest was anything like this—

He wrote an e-mail to Peter Dijkstra asking for a phone number and a time when they could talk.

Peter Dijkstra was not wildly keen on the phone but these things must be done. He gave the number of the hotel and proposed a discussion at 11 am New York time, 5 pm Vienna.

They talked for an hour because Ralph liked to really get to know people before he got to work. "I need to know what you care about," he said. "All the best writers are obsessives."

Peter Dijkstra said, "Well, maybe." If you've been insane you mainly try not to let things get to you, but this was not necessarily a good thing to say to an agent. He said, "Actually, you know, there's one thing. I really like the fact that "front seat" is a spondee. And it's reflected in the spelling, the two separate words. And one thing I really hate is the way they try to make you agree to "backseat," which is obviously trochaic. I *don't* agree. I don't pronounce it as a trochee, I pronounce it as a spondee, and I always spell it as a spondee, "back seat," which has the additional virtue of being logical. But then there were these ridiculous arguments."

"Uh huh, well, I don't remember that coming up in the pages you sent me, but if it's an issue we can definitely deal with it. Send me everything you have," said Ralph. He wanted to get cracking.

You'd think it wouldn't be that big a deal, but actually typing a text always felt like this thing you see a lot in Britain, especially in terraced houses, this practice of replacing a small front garden with a slab of concrete. It was apparently quite a common part of "doing up" a house. You would ride a bus down a long terrace of lower middle class houses, and the ones that were freshly painted and plastered all had a square of cement where the garden had been.

At the same time, oddly enough, once the thing was typed it was up for grabs. If you wrote something in a notebook the words just were the marks your pen or pencil left on the paper, but once they were typed into Word people could smuggle in the unspeakable trochaic "backseat" behind your back.

Of course, if you want those words in a notebook to be a solution to credit card debt, there is a bridge that has to be crossed. But if you don't want to crack up you have to be pretty careful. But again this is probably not a good thing to say.

What he did was he seized on a phrase.

Somewhere online he had come across the phrase "protective of his work."

It had struck him as the height of banality at the time, but for that very reason the kind of thing someone who "fell in love with a book" would probably take to.

So he wrote an e-mail using the phrase "protective of my work" and promised to send the book when it was finished.

He went out for a beer, because it was restful hearing the Austrians rattle words off their sharp metal tongues. He was gone for some time.

When he got back—it was 4 in the morning or so—he found the phrase had hit the jackpot. Not only had Ralph taken to it, he had been galvanized into talking about the few magical pages in hand to everyone he knew. A magazine had offered $5,000 to publish them as a self-contained story. "I understand that you are protective of your work"—it was a lucky thing that this was conveyed in an e-mail rather than over the phone, as it did not matter that he burst out laughing—"but it would be a real wake-up call for publishers." A number of startling proposals followed: if authorized to do so, Ralph would ask the publisher of the novellas and stories (long out of print) to "revert the rights," so that they could then be "bundled" with the new book when put up for auction. This would then trigger a push to translate the five novels immured in their native Dutch; the 1,000-page killer whale could be the next *2666*!

Of course, this is the European fantasy of an American. When other languages need a word for a go-getter they use the word "go-getter," which is the quintessential American thing to be.

If you have been insane there are so many things you can't do.

He was able to write a brief e-mail of thanks and acceptance. He felt that he should say something along the lines of Dear Ralph, This is very exciting, but this he was not able to do.

Based on the two pages he had read, he was not a big fan of *2666*.

He went outside and smoked a Marlboro.

He went inside and downstairs and lay down on the white bed.

Ralph too had seized on a phrase, "the next *2666*."

He used the phrase in an impetuous conversation with Cissy, who said, "Oh, I didn't know you knew Dutch."

"No no no," Ralph said hastily, impatiently. "Something tells me I'm on the right track. For God's sake don't mention it to anyone who does, it might get back to the Eldridges. I'm just wrapping up reversion of rights, we don't want them going behind our backs to Meulenhoff and picking up something else on the cheap."

"Oh, okay," said Cissy. Maybe there was an article on Words Without Borders or something.

Ralph made a vague soothing affectionate noise about her

book and got off the phone and was soon talking to Rachel, who had seen the pages and loved them.

"*Oh*," said Rachel, "I *loved 2666*."

She did not ask if he knew Dutch or had even actually read *2666* because Ralph, the thing he could do was build castles in the air and get people to buy them. If he could build a castle in the air for Peter Dijkstra the genius would fly on a magic carpet.

"I know he's protective of his work," said Ralph. "I *understand*. And I would *never* do anything to jeopardize the creative process. The work must come first."

Rachel made a vague soothing affectionate noise.

He said, "But sometimes there's a *moment* when people get swept *away*, and if you miss it you're fighting against the fact that it's somebody else's moment. I think this is his moment. This may sound crazy, but I think if I could even just get all the *notebooks* in a room, and let a few select people see them, that would be enough to do a deal. Right now there just isn't enough. Not in today's climate. But if they see there's something substantial actually there, if the quality is there, no, I think that would work. But of course, *aaargh*, I can't ask him to send the originals and copies are impossible so the only solution would be to bring him to New York but I *know*, I *know*, I *know*, he's a very private person, how can you throw someone like that into the media maelstrom?"

All this because Rachel had apprenticed to a master of the vague soothing affectionate noise.

Peter Dijkstra lay on a very white bed with his head on his arm.

This would not do.

The go-getter had e-mailed him several times reiterating that the work must come first. Each iteration came with the rider that if there was anything else he felt able to show, anything at all, they could take advantage of a moment which might not come again.

He leapt suddenly to his feet. He took the notebook from which text had been typed and the file cards from which words had been strung together in the notebook. He placed them in his satchel. He left his room, took the stairs three at a time, strode through the breakfast room and out into the street and around the corner to a shop that sold stationery. He purchased a padded envelope. He placed notebook and file cards in the envelope.

As an afterthought he snatched up a postcard with a photograph of Empress Elisabeth of Austria ("Sisi") and wrote painstakingly on the back: Dear Ralph, This is how it starts out and it has to stay where it starts out until it is ready to end. Regards, P.D.

He sealed the envelope, addressed it, strode storklike to the post office, paid postage for a method of delivery that was a little faster than normal without being exorbitant, handed over the envelope and strode storklike to the street. His head was not at all good but he was not positively stalking down the street saying out *loud* "When you say you know the work must come first what exactly do you *mean*?" That was something.

It was also something that he had not written *Erbarmung!!!!!! Erbarmung!!!!!!!* on the postcard.

It can't be a good idea to implore an agent with heartrending appeals to *Parsifal*.

He lit a Marlboro.

Gil sat on the squashy old sofa, legs akimbo, forearms on thighs. He was wearing a very soft faded bluish t-shirt on which dolphins frolicked around the words DAYTONA BEACH *Florida* and soft faded frayed cut-offs. Rachel sat at the other end of the sofa; she wore the SUDO MAKE ME A SANDWICH t-shirt and soft faded white cut-offs, also frayed. Both were barefoot.

On a battered oak coffee table in front of the sofa were: 20-odd pages of double-spaced type; a basket of bagels with cream cheese and lox; a cafetière of very black coffee; a carton of half-and-half; a carton of grapefruit juice; a few cans of San Pellegrino with orange; a large bottle of Gerolsteiner. Plates, glasses, mugs, knives. Gil had suggested getting together over a late breakfast because he did not feel comfortable drinking vodka in front of Ralph.

A squashy old armchair, brother to the sofa, awaited Ralph. Meanwhile they were alone.

Ralph was late, late enough for Gil to start to hope he would not come.

"This is probably going to sound really precious," said Gil. "But I'm not comfortable with this."

"It's not precious," said Rachel. "*Nobody* is comfortable with Ralph. I mean, I only got into coding in the first place to keep myself sane. I would get off the phone after one of these marathon sessions and just tie myself to Boolean logic like a *mast*. And now that I have Barbara, she's so professional and businesslike, she's like a rock. But maybe. He was in an asylum all those years. If he had a whole book he could take it to Barbara, and it could be all right. But he doesn't have a book. And anyway there would still be the whole thing of getting people whipped up to a frenzy over a Dutch writer, and the whole point of Barbara is she doesn't do frenzy. So maybe frenzy is the price he has to pay to stay in this place Cissy found instead of an asylum. I mean, it could just be that way."

"I guess."

This was what he had always liked, she could sail effortlessly uncomplicatedly through. But he did not think he could tell lies for Peter Dijkstra, and he did not want to find himself somehow underwriting a book in Dutch he had never read as the next *2666*.

The coffee was unreproachfully tepid.

Now that Ralph was living one day at a time he would often spend hours talking some poor desperate soul out of a crisis. You would arrange to meet and find yourself catching up on *Dinosaur Comics* on your iPhone, checking the time, catching up on *A Softer World*, checking the time, wondering whether there was anything new (*please* say yes, God, *please*) on *Perry Bible Fellowship*, getting a 503 Service Unavailable!!!!!!!, scouring around online to see whether this was permanent or what?????!!!!!!, noticing the time, only to have Ralph walk belatedly in or text or call to explain that Dale or Jane or Andy was suicidal and he had to be there for them. Not that Gil wanted any extra person to be suicidal, but if someone was suicidal anyway and Ralph had to be there for them rather than here for him it would Be. So. Great.

But no, the buzzer buzzed.

Ralph came eagerly down the long room in a glow of happiness, this Tom Cruise "I am a Thetan!!!!!!" kind of glow which, okay, somehow this was less creepy in the days when you knew he was doing drugs? But okay, okay, okay.

He wore a tan polo shirt with a crocodile on the breast, chinos, and sockless Topsiders, because he had never wanted to be a suit.

He took a padded envelope from his bicycle bag. "*Here*," he said, eyes ablaze. "I'm *sorry* I'm late but when you see you'll *see*." He put it at the midpoint of the squashy sofa and sank into the squashy chair. (It was kind of like Joseph Smith presiding over the display of a golden tablet from the Book of Mormon.)

Gil did not touch the envelope. Rachel picked it up and removed a notebook and a pack of some 70 file cards. She handed the notebook to Gil and began reading through the grid-ruled file cards, one by one.

Ralph gave them a lot of space to read in silence. It was weird holding in your hands things that had been in the hands of Peter Dijkstra, as if the Van Gogh Museum would let you take a painting off the wall. It was kind of weird holding them with Ralph expectantly watching—but no, Ralph suddenly noticed the cold thing of coffee and said ruefully "I *am* late, I'll make fresh" and went off to the kitchen, so fine. Fine.

It's true. You definitely got the feeling, holding these objects, that they had been in a room with a crazy guy, or rather a guy with the potential to be crazy who was trying to keep madness at bay. The writing was small and precise and clear, this slightly pedantic European handwriting that you would normally never see. Reading a typescript, you would miss this: it was like hearing excellent English spoken with a foreign accent. You saw the effort that had gone into the excellence. Precision, a bulwark. (The word "bulwark" was in fact on one of the cards.) You could see that maybe the visibility of the effort had to stay there for the completion, or even the continuation, of the work.

Ralph came back with fresh coffee.

Rachel put each file card back at the midpoint of the sofa as she finished it.

Ralph did not return to the squashy chair. He poured himself a mug of coffee and wandered tactfully off to browse bookshelves.

An experience you tend not to have at the Van Gogh Museum is of a security guard wandering tactfully off and rummaging through your backpack while you are staring your eyes out at paintings you have only seen in books and calendars and posters.

In some kind of weird activation of peripheral vision Gil not so much saw as sensed Ralph pausing by the 18 inches of shelving dedicated to Peter Dijkstra. Which was a good 13 inches more than were taken up by the stories and the novellas.

Gil had met Rachel in the gift shop of the Van Gogh Museum in the heat of the hype. She had picked up a paperback, *Vincent Van Gogh, een leven in brieven.*

He had seen her across a room but kept his distance. If you have never been to Amsterdam before and maybe never will be again you don't want to smear the paintings with a lot of boy-meets-girl stuff. There were paintings on the walls that had been in a room with a crazy guy, a guy who never sold any paintings; you want to be alone with the craziness. He walked from room to room, seeing her across each room, keeping his distance.

The gift shop did seem like this space designed to ease the transition to the world of men.

She saw him and held up the book and smiled. (They had been so many places at the same time, it was like running into someone at the mall who was in five of your classes.) He asked if she knew Dutch. She said, "No, but maybe it's better that way. It's as if there were special words for colors that nobody else had ever used. *Koningsblauw*—I don't even know how you say it, but maybe I just want to know it exists." She showed him a page on which he saw the word *Sterrennacht*.

They did not agree to leave together but they left together. As they passed a bookshop Gil said "Wait!" and ran in and bought five books by Peter Dijkstra that had not been translated, because he might never be in Amsterdam again and he had to have them. If he had not met her it would never have occurred to him to buy books he could not read and probably never would and yet had to have.

Neither of them was stupid enough to tell anyone, even close friends, because you never know who will say something to someone and then it is out in the world, something that meant something all cartoonified and fatuous. But he looked at the pages of the notebook and thought of the Van Gogh Museum and keeping his distance and running into the bookstore.

He did not want to share this with Ralph and he also did not want Ralph to leap to conclusions re his apparent immersion in the oeuvre and suddenly it seemed it had to be one or the other.

Gil finished the notebook before Rachel finished the file cards. He put it at the midpoint of the sofa and picked up the file cards she had finished and when she had finished the file cards she picked up the notebook and when they had both finished they put the things in their hands back at the midpoint of the sofa.

Ralph returned to the squashy chair. "You *see*," he said simply. "You *see*." He said he had e-mailed Peter and asked how many more notebooks there were and there were about 50. (It was weird hearing him called "Peter.")

He talked again about the moment and what he could do if Peter Dijkstra and his notebooks were brought to New York.

If Ralph had not been there they would have gone on passing the notebook and file cards back and forth in silent wonder. Or maybe one would have said, "Look at this," and the other would have said, "Look at this."

Ralph went on being there.

Instead of "Look at this" they got stuff like, the longer there was no actual deal, no major player with an option on the backlist, the greater the danger that someone would snap up the next *2666* for peanuts.

Gil stood up. He padded down the room to a shoe rack from which he took a pair of socks and a pair of Timberland boots which he slipped on before opening the door. Turning.

He said, "I'm sorry, but I can't— This is too important for me. It would mean a lot to see the other notebooks, if he was willing to show them. If you think it would help, I can pay his airfare to New York and he can stay in the loft and you can show people the notebooks in the loft if that helps and I will move in with Rachel until it's over. But I can't do this other stuff and I can't talk about this anymore."

He closed the door behind him.

"Oh *God*," said Ralph, "I didn't mean—"

Rachel made a vague soothing affectionate noise.

•

Striding barelegged and booted down Vestry Street, down Hudson, Gil had this sudden paranoid image of the 50 notebooks, these Van Goghy *things*, these things it would be transcendent to sit quietly down with, on a big table in his loft with the five Dutch books placed inconspicuously by as if to *imply* without Gil even saying a word that he had read them in the original Dutch (such being his fanatical devotion to the genius) and could vouch for King Kong being the next *2666*. This or that editor being ushered in and not even having the books pointed out by Ralph because they'd just quietly accidentally be *there*. But this was totally paranoid, right? *Right*? Because *nobody* would do something that icky, would they? *Would* they? Or should he take them to Rachel's to be on the safe side? Or would giving in to paranoia make it worse? Or—

The Timberlands had propelled him east on Worth. They crossed West Broadway, turned south. He was just thinking that maybe he would do something totally normal such as go to Edward's for a hamburger and fries, Edward's being a block away, when he saw, sitting dreamily outside at Edward's, Miss Total Weirdness. He sidestepped into the nearest doorway. Which turned out to be that (the Lord is my shepherd, I shall not want) of a bar. It was maybe not totally normal to have a double vodka at 12:02, but fuck it.

One of the very few benefits of fame was that the bartender recognized him, so it did not matter that he had come out without any money.

Peter Dijkstra had recently discovered a nice fact. There is a German word, *getigert*, for a cat with striped fur. This immediately transforms one's view of the animal. (This small domestic tiger.) This had led to other nice facts: the verb, *tigern*, means an activity which corresponds to the English words *mooch, loiter* (this on the authority of pons.eu), the French word *flâner*, all surely with radically different connotations from the Dutch word *lanterfanten*. A lord of the jungle, off the prowl, proceeding as chance takes him velvet-pawed through his domain, twitching his lordly tail—this is quite different, clearly, from, well, *lanterfanten* is also the word which goes into the English for *fiddle while Rome burns*. And a *flâneur*, this is Baudelaire, this is an inhabitant of Walter Benjamin's *Passagenwerk*, the *Arcades Project*. Jeepers!

He wrote *getigert!!!!!* on one file card and *tigern, mooch, loiter, flâner, lanterfanten*, and *lummelen* on another. At the bottom of the second file card he wrote *Sp? It?* And, presently: *bighellonare?*

Gil ordered a second Potocki and took it to a booth. (He loved booths. But who doesn't love booths?)

The notebooks had, maybe discomfort isn't something you can crystallize, but he felt really uncomfortable.

When he had read Rachel's first book it was not exactly whether it was good or bad, but he wanted to feel he knew the most important thing about her, that every single detail was something she had picked out of the world. But the genius could not be in the details because the details were exactly what Ralph prided himself on attention to. So any detail could always have displaced some other detail, which was the detail Rachel had chosen before the detail attracted attention. How could someone just casually displace that? This was a guy who would pay $100 to have a crocodile on a polo shirt. To say that it wasn't even that he liked crocodiles would be to miss the point, there was no way he would wear any shirt with a crocodile motif even if he *did* like crocodiles, or any shirt with *any* motif, unless it was an emblem you had to pay $100 to have on a shirt.

This had been, maybe "inchoate" is the word. For the unease. (Which was now, what, choate? Really?) He *had* thought he loved

Peter Dijkstra's work when he read the novellas and the stories, but when he saw the notebook and the file cards there was this sudden jolt, because this was English that Peter Dijkstra had actually picked and it was different from the English people had picked to share Peter Dijkstra with English readers.

Which was not a problem in *itself*, because there had always been Dutch words behind the English words someone had picked. Whereas.

Cissy did not want to be paranoid but she sensed that there was an inner circle and she was not in it. Adam did not want to be paranoid. Ellen did not want to be paranoid. Merrill did not want to be paranoid. That is, Cissy sat over steak and frites at Edward's, Adam had an Omelette Ardennaise and a Leffe at Petite Abeille (he *adored* Tintin), Ellen was just mooching up West Broadway toward a grilled cheese on rye at the Square Diner, Merrill was heading for a TBA brunch at the Odeon when they saw Gil duck into a bar, and fame being what it is all four thought he was avoiding them. Fame being what it is a devotion to the work of Peter Dijkstra had looked briefly like the ticket to an inner circle, and *now* look. It was horrible. It was false to everything that had ever mattered about Peter Dijkstra.

Cissy was the one who had followed her instincts and found herself in a hotel like a monastery, *independently chosen* by Peter Dijkstra. Oh, she should go back to following her instincts. She should be true to herself. Passing through Berlin she had seen a restaurant in the Daimler showroom on Unter den Linden; she had thought of having Breakfast at Daimler's and laughed out loud but there was a plane to catch, why had she stupidly caught that plane? She would go back to Berlin and have Breakfast at Daimler's every day among the gleaming classic cars until she had written a book as fast and sleek and gleaming as a Daimler.

Adam had found a place in Cappadocia where the people lived in caves, and *later*, beached in New York, found it independently singled out in the PD novella. Why had he left? He would go to Cappadocia and live in a room in a hotel in a cave until he had written a book of cavedwellers in a windwashed land.

Ellen had once missed a flight in Istanbul and spent 12 hours in the food mezzanine, an expanse of white plastic tables as far as the eye could see. There was a Burger King and a bar and a deli serving authentic Turkish food, and that day among the white tables was the best of her life. Why had she stupidly boarded her plane? (Peter Dijkstra would not have boarded the plane.) She would go back to Istanbul and stay at the airport and write a book as unencumbered and directionless as a room of white plastic tables.

Merrill had once stayed in a worn-down hotel in Paris, the Hôtel Tiquetonne, in a tiny room on the seventh floor, and he had been happy. Peter Dijkstra would have stayed, taking the creaking elevator with its accordion iron door. He would go and he would write a book as lighthearted in a worn-down world as a room in a downtrodden hotel on the seventh floor.

Perhaps this was not what Ralph had in mind when he talked of the passing of the moment, and yet the moment was passing.

Gil felt the confines of the inner circle closing in around him.

The way to be true to Peter Dijkstra was to be true to himself.

A loft and stuff is the kind of thing that fits into the *transaction* of the gift, you can *transfer, bestow*. But *not* having a loft and stuff, solitude, silence, being alone in a room with a notebook, if you *have* these things you can't give them by transferring or bestowing.

Peter Dijkstra was in this four-room underground hotel in Vienna and he had filled 50 notebooks and if he could fill 50 notebooks why would he want to do anything but stay in the underground hotel filling notebooks? Why would he want a loft and somebody else's stuff?

But what if???!!!!!

What if the normal rate for a room at this underground hotel is $79 a night, BUT, you could get a room with notebooks & file cards on loan from Peter Dijkstra for $299 a night, and the $220 goes to Peter Dijkstra. So he can keep his room indefinitely because it is paid for out of lending out his notebooks &c. AND. There are SEPARATE ENTRANCES. So you NEVER SEE Peter Dijkstra. He uses one entrance and you use another, so he can go on working without interruption, and you can sit in your room with the notebooks. This would Be. So. Great.

It would be great if you knew Peter Dijkstra's favorite restaurants. People go to the restaurant and they can just order a meal. *Or*, they can order a meal plus notebook and file cards for the cost of an extra meal, which is left on account for Peter Dijkstra. Who can turn up whenever he wants and find his meal is already paid for!

Gil could totally see himself going to a restaurant and ordering a meal and a notebook and paying extra for the notebook. It would be better than going to a restaurant and having a meal with Peter Dijkstra and paying for the meal because there was no reason to think words from the mouth would have the intensity of the ink on the grid.

He asked the bartender for a napkin and a pen, and he scribbled down the ideas in their brilliance as fast as they came.

He would write a book in which people did not destroy the thing they loved.

Peter Dijkstra got an e-mail from the go-getter the gist of which was that the notebook and file cards had struck a bonanza. A young writer who worshipped his work had offered the use of his loft and airfare and if he would take his notebooks to New York editors would make an exception and read the work in this unpolished state and the go-getter could virtually guarantee that they could get a deal on the strength of this and set the ball rolling.

He got an e-mail from the young American proposing schemes which seemed to involve encouraging total strangers to descend on his hotel and favorite restaurants and go through his papers.

He got e-mails from one young American after another who had learned to be true to themselves.

Peter Dijkstra had been sitting at the small desk in his room. He stood up, stretched. He left the room, went upstairs and went out into the street. It was not a very nice street: one good thing about the rooms was the fact that they had no view.

He could not think of anything to say in reply to the e-mails. Or rather, what he wanted to say was, "I'm a very good man, but I'm a very bad wizard."

He lit a Marlboro and went off in search of a beer or maybe a Sachertorte or a schnitzel. He could not say which verb described the movement of his aimless feet.

Improvisation Is the Heart of Music

'The rest was pure Arabian Nights. Gazelle-eyed maidens with perfumed robes brought inlaid boxes of Turkish delight and roast hummingbirds and sugared grapes and honeyed wine—ghastly stuff—and tiny cups of sludgy coffee. Silks kissed the earth. Our host raised his hands and clapped—once—twice—three times, and on the third the strains of a harp wafted in from the wings.

'"But my dear chaps! You're not eating!" he cried. "Try the hummingbirds, I assure you they are excellent. Or a morsel of lamb? And you must, you positively must sample the mare's milk cheese, it is a speciality of my people, a great delicacy. Fatima! See that the gentlemen have some cheese!"

'He went on in this way for some time, and after I suppose half an hour or so said—"But come! I shall order them to prepare us a hookah, and my companions shall entertain you. Which did you favour among those who served you?"

'Now I was prepared to see what the hookah was like, and even—dare I confess it?—be entertained by one of the companions, at least up to a point. But Angus is a true Scot, his Presbyterian blood curdled at the sound of this.

'"Of course I'll not touch his filthy hookah," he whispered to me in tones just loud enough not to be tactful.

'Our host went on with the utmost urbanity, as though nothing had been said, urging us to express a preference for one of the girls. Angus preserved the silence of outraged virtue. I murmured something noncommittal, all extremely attractive, impossible to choose one above the rest. This, it turned out, was a bad move.

'"My dear fellow—" he cut me short "—I understand perfectly—to tell the truth I'm not, myself, entirely in the mood—as your friend's tastes, it seems, are not in that direction (he smiled rather maliciously at poor Angus, who went bright red as only a rufus can)—you shall have them all!" A barrage of claps, and a bevy (it really is the only word for it, echt B movie stuff) of beautiful girls surrounded me, urging me to recline on a sort of divan strewn with silk rugs and shawls dripping with fringe.

'Mahmet excused himself with a profound bow, leaving me, I took it, to disport myself with the company provided. If this was his object the ruse failed dismally, since he neglected to take Angus with him. Angus continued to sit bolt upright on his cushion, pulled out his pocket copy of Thompson's *Making of the English Working Class* in a battered old blue and white Pelican edition, and buried himself in its pages, the picture of dour intellectual respectability. It effectively cast a damper on the debaucheries in which I was supposed to be rejoicing at the other end of the tent. After a little laboured banter with the beauties I sent them off, pulled out my Edmund Crispin, and started reading—it was the final humiliation to have nothing better to show than a humble green and white Penguin.

'We turned in soon after. We never saw our host again: in the morning the Nubian appeared with a message on a tray. I took it, and he disappeared without a word. It was from Mahmet:

'"My dear chaps,

Business calls me away unexpectedly. So sorry to interrupt our larks together! Please avail yourselves of the yacht for as long as convenient. What a story for your grandchildren! You can tell them you were once shipwrecked with

Sindbad the Sailor"'

Edward paused dramatically before the name; after pronouncing it he fell silent, ending the story with a resounding close. He leant back into the corner of the sofa with a little expectant smile. The silence stretched out, a little awkwardly. As always with Edward's stories, a round of applause seemed the most fitting response, but this is seldom used other than ironically in private conversation. Maria had not yet worked out an acceptable substitute, though she had had plenty of opportunity to practice: Edward was a gifted raconteur. Edward and Maria were engaged, but without the ease this implies—Maria still found herself struggling to keep up with a companion of such wonderfully polished conversational skills. What *was* the appropriate response to narrative tours de force? Should one praise the performance? Aim for intelligent comment? Laugh? Counter with a story of one's own? That reminds me of the time I—but Maria's life offered little in the way of anecdotal material, none of Edward's stories had any connection with the sort of thing that happened to her.

'What a story!' she exclaimed. 'I've always wanted to hear a genuine traveller's tale: you don't happen to have a bit of Roc's egg lying about, I suppose?'

'Nary a one—I did think the least our host could do was leave us each a ruby the size of an orange, but Sindbad seems to be a bit of a Thatcherite these days.'

Maria laughed heartily.

Edward and Maria had a big wedding. Maria had a very pretty dress (lace over satin); she decided to have a *long* veil. The men wore morning suits. She had a little going-away suit in nubbly pink silk, with binding, just the least bit Chanel, and a little hat. How can you have that kind of wedding and not be just the tiniest bit camp? Edward and Maria got in the limo amid showers of rice and confetti. Edward laughed, and kissed her. 'You look lovely, my dear.'

•

They were taking a real old-fashioned honeymoon! They would go to Paris by boat-train, spend a week there, then go south to the Riviera. They would spend two weeks on a cruise ship, stopping first at various Italian ports, then at the Greek islands. They sat side by side in their compartment, holding hands—it was not something they had done often.

'Y'know, I hope I have better luck this time than the last time I went sailing,' said Edward.

'Why is that?' asked Maria.

'The last time I went sailing I got shipwrecked! Have I ever told you the story? It was when Angus McBride and I went island hopping after Finals. Altogether a fantastic tale! We'd booked onto something that sounded perfectly respectable—the Hellenic Swan or some such thing—but turned out to be a great tub of a Victorian yacht that had been restored and put to work for the tourist trade. Amazing boat! Someone had clearly done it up to the nines about eighty years ago. Plush upholstery—swags of gold rope—thick Turkey carpets—vast numbers of cut-glass chandeliers—and a lot of brass and mahogany woodwork. It was all rather the worse for wear by the time it crossed our path, and its owners hadn't had much luck in luring tourists aboard—the only other passenger was a mysterious Turk! Well, we'd only just started to make his acquaintance by the tarnished grandeur of the bar, when we ran into a bit of rough weather in the Adriatic, and the bloody boat started to go down!

'Mahmet got us rather briskly into one of the lifeboats and winched us down. Then Angus and I started rowing like blazes! We saw the crew pulling off in another boat. We'd got perhaps a couple of hundred yards away when we saw the ship go under. I don't suppose I've ever seen such a terrifying sight. One moment rather a lot of the bow and a fair bit of cabin roof were still above water; then an enormous swell rose above it, and the whole she-bang was sucked under in a couple of seconds. A few flecks of foam and a stray life preserver were left floating on the surface where, just a few minutes earlier, there'd been a twelve-ton yacht.

'We were at sea in the lifeboat until noon the next day. Angus and I had already started wondering whether it might be prudent to ration supplies, but Mahmet was superbly unconcerned. In the event we could have gorged on the water biscuits and tinned luncheon meats in the hold: we were picked up by a magnificent yacht which turned out to belong to Mahmet. He'd been on his way south to meet it at Genoa, but its captain had had the sense to head north when he heard of the disaster which had befallen the Swan. We were shown to a cabin, where we slept heavily all the afternoon—we hadn't got much sleep the night before. When we woke we found we were at anchor off an unidentifiable bit of coast. A gigantic Nubian told us we were to join Mahmet on shore for dinner, and saw us into a small motorboat. We were taken ashore, and escorted into a vast tent which had been set up on the sand.

'The rest was pure Arabian Nights. Gazelle-eyed maidens with perfumed robes brought Turkish delight in inlaid boxes and roast hummingbirds and sugared grapes and honeyed wine—ghastly stuff—and tiny cups of sludgy coffee. Silks kissed the earth. Our host raised his hands and clapped—once—twice—three times, and on the third the strains of a harp wafted in from the wings.'

Edward raised his hands and clapped; paused; clapped; paused; clapped again, and then caressed, gracefully, the air with his right hand in a wavy glide suggestive of the delicate notes of the harp.

'"But my dear chaps! You're not eating!" he cried. "Try the hummingbirds, I assure you they are excellent. Or a morsel of lamb? And you must, you positively must sample the mare's milk cheese, it is a speciality of my people, a great delicacy. Fatima! See that the gentlemen have some cheese!"'

Maria crossed her legs, shifted on her seat, held her elbows. She had been, from time to time, slightly put out by Edward's habit of modulating out of dialogue into anecdote, but she had supposed it to be, at least, a matter of spontaneous impulse. This mechanical repetition was something quite other and alarming.

'We turned in soon after. We never saw our host again: in the morning the Nubian appeared with a message on a tray. I took it, and he disappeared without a word. It was from Mahmet:

'"My dear chaps,

Business calls me away unexpectedly. So sorry to interrupt our larks together! Please avail yourselves of the yacht for as long as convenient. What a story for your grandchildren! You can tell them you were once shipwrecked with

Sindbad the Sailor"'

Edward paused dramatically before the name, and after pronouncing it fell silent, ending the story with a resounding close. He leant back into the corner of the compartment with a little expectant smile. Maria smiled back nervously. So well-rehearsed a performance seemed to call more than ever for applause. What conversational alternatives were there? Would it be acceptable to repeat her comments of last time? Would Edward recognise them, and realise that he had told her the story before? Maria felt that this would be hideously embarrassing. She must come up with something new. At the same time it seemed unfair: *she* must improvise because he had rehearsed.

Perhaps it was a matter of rehearsing conversations until one got them right. Perhaps she had not responded well enough last time, so that Edward had had a niggling sense that a proper performance of story and reception had not taken place; perhaps this was her chance to improve. This was an alarming thought: if she did not rise to the occasion, the story might be brought out again and again until she perfected her reply.

'What a marvellous story!' she exclaimed hastily. 'I've always adored *The Count of Monte Cristo*—there's a wonderful Dumasian quality about this, isn't there, the European swept suddenly from the midst of the working day technological world into the fantastic improbabilities of the Orient!'

'Yes,' said Edward, smiling agreeably, 'one did rather feel that one had been catapulted into a big baggy monster of romantic French historicism. Thoroughly enjoyable for someone with low tastes like me, but a terrible trial for poor Angus, who felt he'd done nothing to deserve it. He stalked off the yacht at the earliest possible opportunity, injured innocence writ large on his brow.'

The Rapide hurtled through France. It was night; the windows of the compartment showed Edward and Maria only themselves surrounded by the paraphernalia of travel: the *Spectator*, some paperback mysteries, one of the Lucia books (Maria was not yet enough at ease to buy herself *Vogue*); a partially eaten Cadbury's Fruit and Nut bar, a packet of Jaffa cakes, a couple of oranges; a thermos flask of tea. The hours of travel had been punctuated by the recounting of anecdotes, many of them familiar to Maria. After each story Maria would pick up a theme for comment in the counterpoint which must follow; Edward would develop it briefly, then silence would fall. Sometimes Maria would bring out a new subject, which would be canvassed for a few moments before it reminded Edward of another story. Sometimes they turned to each other and smiled, and kissed, abandoning the struggle to converse.

•

The morning brought other pleasures. They sat in the dining car, looking at each other brightly across a table with a cloth. A waiter brought croissants and a pot of very strong coffee. They reached eagerly for croissants, for jam, drank coffee, set their cups down with a little sigh.

'Why is it, do you suppose,' said Edward, 'that the Continental breakfast has only to cross the Channel to be so damp and depressing. It *seems* simple enough—why does it travel so badly? In England one wonders whether it is really meant to be eaten. Here it is invariably ambrosial.'

'It is the tyranny of the toast rack,' said Maria. 'No self-respecting bed and breakfast can be without them; and once you've invested in the technology you're *committed* to sliced white. But if you offer croissants and pastries of course no one will touch the white toast, so no one ever does offer anything else. They feel they must get a return on their investment.'

'There is something in what you say,' said Edward. 'But that doesn't account for everything. Why are croissants in England so awful? You never mind not having them because they taste like limp cardboard anyway.'

The subject of food is like Chopsticks: almost anyone can improvise on it. Two people who devise variations on something simple and silly end of course by collapsing into laughter: Edward and Maria smiled at each other in relief.

The yacht was comfortable, nothing remarkable. The islands, of course, were enchanting. They'd go for walks in the morning, not *too* early, taking a picnic lunch; stop at the beach, spread towels, eat brown olives and feta and yellow tomatoes and funny bread, drink retsina or local plonk; spend the afternoons swimming in the limpid water.

Edward had been there before and had lots of stories: about German tourists solemnly pacing through an olive grove at Mystras, heads popping up and down as they consulted an archaeological guide, sneering at the merely Byzantine and poking about for a few dusty stones of Sparta; of Americans looking haplessly round the local taverna, speaking wistfully of McDonald's; of the plausible scoundrel who'd wanted only to open a high-class tourist shop in Rhodes, to sell genuine local handicrafts made in Taiwan.

Maria smiled and laughed. Everything was new to her.

'Oh look!' she cried; it was a fat old woman in black with a mule and a CD Walkman; it was a gnarled old man in Nikes with a sheep round his neck; it was a couple of very beautiful young men in very tight Calvin Klein jeans, 'and they say there's no such thing as Platonic love! Alive and well and on the strut in the agora, wouldn't you say?'

But it was hard to be perfectly at ease.

Novelty disturbed Edward; he made an awkward remark or two about the old woman, was only happy when he had been reminded of one he saw years ago and could supply a polished little story for the occasion. Repetition disturbed Maria; it was like trying to play jazz with someone who has the sheet music for 'Ain't Misbehavin'' and works it in whenever he can.

They met a couple of college pals of Edward's in Lesbos, and took them back to the yacht for dinner.

'Not very grand, but perfectly seaworthy,' Edward said agreeably, leaping to the deck from the pier. 'One learns to appreciate these things. Did I ever tell you of the time I was shipwrecked?'

If he had no one would admit to it.

'Oh, it was yonks ago, when Angus McBride and I went island hopping after Finals,' said Edward, leading the way to the bar. '(What can I get you? I think we've got all the usual.) Altogether a fantastic tale! We'd booked onto something that sounded perfectly respectable—the Hellenic Swan or some such thing—but turned out to be a great tub of a Victorian yacht which had been restored and put to work for the tourist trade...'

Edward and Maria return to the little house they have bought in Leckford Road, Maria trailing the past behind her. Every conversation she has had, every story she has heard, is on record in her phonographic memory, and on record also are the responses made by all the people she has ever known, and the records of her friendships are the most complete. Perhaps friendships are a matter of similar collections: you have the original, the friend has a backup. Her conversations with Edward are all on record, but hers is the only copy.

Edward bounds gaily into the house, the happy wanderer with his little light backpack of essentials, and she follows him slowly, carrying the luggage.

'Shall we have some people to dinner for a housewarming?' she asks, and sees her words thin into the air like vapour off early morning water.

'Oh, yes, we must,' says Edward, and they do.

Edward and Maria sit at opposite ends of the dining room table, and between them are six or seven friends. They fill glasses, urge seconds, swap honeymoon anecdotes—the friends are married, they have their share.

'A yacht,' says Sarah. 'Crumbs. George and I went Eurorail! You must have felt frightfully grand.'

Edward opens his mouth.

'Oh,' says Maria, 'Edward was sickeningly blasé. One really felt it was an awful come-down for him. Have you ever told them about the splendour amidst which you were shipwrecked, darling?'

Everyone has gone, and Edward and Maria repair to the kitchen to tackle the washing up. Edward scrapes and stacks; Maria fills the basin with Fairy Liquid and steaming water. As she lets the first stack of dishes sink beneath the suds she begins to sing softly.

'o when the saints, o when the saints, o when the saints come marching in'

'how i long to be in that number,' sings Edward, 'when the saints come marching in.'

'O WHEN THE SAINTS. O WHEN THE SAINTS. O WHEN THE SAINTS COME MARCHING IN! HOW I LONG — TO — BE — INTHATNUMBER, O WHEN THE SAINTS COME MARCHING IN.'

o when the saints (o when the saints) come marching in (come marching in) o when the saints come marching (marching in), how I long to be in that nu-u-mber. When the saints come marching in.

OXFORD, 1985

Famous Last Words

'Structuralism is out of fashion anyway,' says Brian, who likes to be a kind of thinking man's Philistine. He slides a spoon into raspberry sorbet.

'Post-structuralism is out of fashion,' says Jane. They're married, it isn't really surprising.

'Fashion is out of fashion,' says X, in the tone of voice that makes you think 'quipped'.

'Fashion is out of structuralism,' say I. It's nice when they leave you the best line. X doesn't like it, though. Didn't see it coming.

'I liked that pasta alla Gorgonzola,' I say to Jane. 'Is it really so easy? How do you do it?'

Cross looks round the table. I blush, as so often. It was an *intellectual* conversation. Jane doesn't want to answer, she resents being dragged down to this level.

'Oh, you improvise like mad,' she says airily. 'Gorgonzola and sheep's yoghurt are the only essentials.'

This is not very helpful, but I don't like to press her. Brian starts telling stories about Derrida: perfectly happy, it seems, to accept all the privileges of the author. Theories of authorial absence, says Brian, tend to leave out the curious circumstance that the author is always there to pick up his cheque.

X does not seem to resent this. X says as a matter of fact Derrida is a stickler about copyright.

I've finished my sorbet. I finish my coffee. I start thinking about the death of Voltaire.

•

X and I have a long way to walk home afterwards—X lives up the Abingdon Road, I live in Osney. It's about midnight when we leave, and the Woodstock Road is deserted but well-lit: the road is pocked and blackened like a battered sheet of gold, the chestnut trees are brassy.

'Brian is such a wanker,' says X. 'blaBLAblaBLAblaBLA—gossip gossip gossip.'

'Lucky Brian,' say I. I scoop up a handful of dust from a driveway and let it sift through my fingers on the wind. 'The streets are paved with gold.'

X cheers up suddenly. 'Still, I think I made a good impression. You can't ignore politics.'

We cross Leckford Road.

'I was thinking about the death of the author,' I say. 'People use "*la mort de l'auteur*" like "*la mort de Dieu*". I mean, to describe the disintegration—no, the devaluation—the *discrediting* of a concept. It's metaphysical. Nobody thinks God actually died: they think it was never alive in the first place. I think Barthes actually says somewhere "*l'Auteur, lorsqu'on y croit!*" Putting it that way is a paradox—how does a universal die, anyway?'

'Dunno,' says X. 'Kind of obvious, innit?' X sometimes likes to be a Philistine's Philistine.

'The life of the author in Barthes is a matter of being paid too much attention. Death would just be being ignored. No more *Paris Review* interviews—no more of those weird questions. "Do you write on the typewriter?" "Do you write to a schedule?" "When did you start to write?" "Does it come easily?" "Was it hard for you to write about oral sex?" Leon Edel—Leslie Marchand—André Maurois—Gordon Haight—will languish unread on the shelves.'

'Kind of a Berkeleian non-existence,' says X, going along with it. 'There's no one to think of the author but God, and God's dead.'

'But,' I say, 'that leaves you with the death of the author. There are what we could call, for the sake of argument, impostors—people who have deathbeds. There is a sense in which the death of the author is incompatible with "*la mort de l'auteur*". Think of somebody like Voltaire. There's something strangely fascinating about the way everyone tried to write his death.'

X holds up a finger, and says in a strong Cockney accent:

'An orphan's curse would drag to hell
A spirit from on high,
But oh! More horrible than that
Is the curse in a dead man's eye!
Seven days, seven nights I saw that curse
And yet I could not die.—

'Your basic author,' says X, 'is transfixed by the eye of the dead God. What you're talking about,' says X, 'is the night of the Living Dead.'

I think this is clever, but, allowing for the accent, it's the kind of thing Brian might have said.

'But it's interesting,' say I. 'It's a different slant on the question of sincerity. Not, "What did you really mean?" but "Would you still say it?" Recantation …' I say it emphatically, it's a word I expect to appeal to X.

'Authority …' X says thoughtfully.

'Exactly. This idea of getting the one who said it first to take it back—or stick to it! More words from the same source. It's this business of validation, or invalidation, coming from a particular direction—'

'Parsifal!' says X. '*Die Wunde schließt der Speer nur, der sie schlug.*'

'Eh?' (I can read German, but it never seems to sound the way it looks.)

'The wound must be healed by the spear that made it.'

'*Yes*. And I think there's something very striking about the candidates for deathbed conversions: intensely rational, articulate, revolutionary people—Voltaire and Hume. As if no one could be sure of their own arguments unless they could get Voltaire or Hume to repeat them. All these deathbed confessions of Voltaire— it's hard to say what's more interesting, the multiple last statements or the endless arguments about them. Which was genuine? Why did he refuse the sacrament? I've got this book at home, *La religion de Voltaire*, that gets incredibly anxious about it.'

'Sounds interesting,' says X.

'Oh, it is. Pomeau thinks the confessions are tongue in cheek— he goes through them word by word. Which of course simply shows the futility of the exercise—the very problems of sincerity, of interpretative validity, which were to be settled at last without possibility of revision, are all to be settled again for the "final words".'

'I wouldn't mind having a look at that,' says X.

'I'll have to show it to you some time,' say I.

'It's not that late,' says X. 'I can come by your place.'

'Oh,' say I. 'Oh, OK.'

My place is very small. I have use of the kitchen, and a room on the second floor with a narrow view of the canal and swans. X and I sit at the kitchen table, surrounded by books about deaths of authors. I have Noyes' biography of Voltaire, and Pomeau, both with extensive discussions of the death of Voltaire. Noyes also includes a description of a visit to Voltaire by Boswell. Besides these I have the volume of Boswell's journals which includes his interview with the dying Hume. I say that I think I once read something somewhere about the death of Foucault, but I can't remember where.

'The thing that interests me,' I say. 'One of the things that interest me is the way there is this emphasis on inserting the body of the writer into the scene, as if making a connection between this physical presence and the *derniers mots* will somehow make these specially valid. Look at Noyes.' I pick up the book.

'"We must obviously not picture him here with the 'eternal grin' of Mr Lytton Strachey, but with the blood-stained rag at his lips, and eyes that had been looking into the face of Death. Those eyes are turned for a moment, with the curious wonder which is a sick man's only way of reproach, upon a secretary who is trying to defeat a purpose definitely decided upon before this illness occurred."

'The blood-stained rag,' I say, 'says this is real and true. The document is genuine. Its statements may be *attached* to Voltaire.'

X is flipping through Pomeau.

I start rehearsing facts and dates. On February 26, 1778 Voltaire took confession and signed a statement: *Je meurs dans la Religion Catholique où je suis né, espérant de la miséricorde divine, qu'elle daignera pardonner toutes mes fautes, et que si j'avais jamais scandalisé l'Eglise, j'en demande pardon à Dieu et à elle.'* He refused to take the Sacrament because he was spitting up blood and might 'spit up something else' (the exact words are disputed). On February 28 he issued the following statement: *'Je meurs en adorant Dieu, en aimant mes amis, en ne haïssant mes ennemis, et en détestant la superstition.'* At the time of his death, he was attended by the curé of Saint-Sulpice, La Harpe, and Prince Bariatinsky. The curé asked whether he recognised the divinity of Jesus Christ. Voltaire replied, *'Laissez-moi mourir en paix.'*

X has found Pomeau's analysis of the confession. 'Wouldn't take the sacrament—says he dies in the church, not a member of it—second statement the real Voltaire—Whew! *"Il était mort en théiste, non en chrétien."'*

'Whereas Noyes,' say I, 'says Voltaire's early religious training gave him a strong sense of the sanctity of the host.'

X puts a hand on my knee.

'Boswell sounded Voltaire out on immortality,' I say. 'Boswell wore his flowered velvet at the interview. Noyes smiles up his sleeve at this: if the bloody rag is the mark of intellectual commitment, the flowered velvet is that of silly Scottish dilettantism. Boswell asks whether immortality is not a noble idea. Voltaire agrees, but thinks it more desirable than likely. "*Potius optandum quam probandum*" —isn't that a great line? On Voltaire's authority, Boswell goes to see Voltaire's doctor for confirmation that Voltaire had never been afraid of death.'

I look for this in Noyes, and read: '"Had he any horror of it?" "No! The more seriously ill he is, the better Deist he becomes ..." "Ah, well," says Boswell, "I can say all that, then, on the best authority. M. de Voltaire bade me ask you whether he feared death, as ministers of religion had affirmed."'

X and I are smiling. We are both charmed by the flowered velvet. X's hand moves up my thigh. I have noticed this tendency to reductionism in X before. The text is infinitely variegated, the subtext always the same. I tried once to resist this by accusing X of believing in final causes—that for the sake of which the rest is there—but it didn't work. X said I took everything personally. X takes nothing personally: X discussed the deconstruction of teleology and put a hand on my knee.

What is a subtext? You may think of it as a movement in the circumambient language, whose presence you divine by distortions and ripples in the text; what lies between the lines is as invisible, as plain to the eye as the breeze which stirs the leaves of the copper beech in the quadrangle, the high wind that toppled trees in Hyde Park. And we know that the disruption is not in one direction only: the text is a kind of windbreak.

One walks quicker with the wind at one's back. I feel the subtext pushing us forward, and I am rather afraid it will outstrip the text altogether, before I have got to Boswell and Hume, so that—although I could say a good deal more about the 'solemn and singular conversation'—I hasten to open *Boswell in Extremes, 1776–78,* and bring to X's attention Boswell's recollections of the day when he was too late for church, and went to see David Hume who was a-dying.

'"I found him alone, in a reclining posture in his drawing-room. He was lean, ghastly, and quite of an earthy appearance. He was dressed in a suit of grey cloth with white metal buttons, and a kind of scratch wig. He was quite different from the plump figure which he used to present."

'You see what I mean,' I say, '—the physical presence, with its marks of imminent dissolution, guarantees the seriousness of the speaker—at the same time that it threatens permanent absence of the speaker. This, it says, is your last chance to find out what he really thought.'

'Yeh,' says X. 'Basically it's your capitalist perspective on meaning as property: authorial presence can be bequeathed to some textual children—others may be disinherited. Boswell's hoping for a bit of melodrama—a deathbed scene where the *Treatise* and *Enquiry* are cut out of the will.' X squeezes my thigh.

I read rapidly:

'"I had a strong curiosity to be satisfied if he persisted in disbelieving in a future state even when he had death before his eyes. I was persuaded from what he now said, and from his manner of saying it, that he did persist. I asked him if it was not possible that there might be a future state. He answered it was possible that a piece of coal put upon the fire would not burn."'

'Straight out of the *Enquiry,*' says X. 'If Hume had had a Pomeau he'd have been cheering. *Il était mort en athéiste non en théiste.*'

'The bulk of my estate,' say I, 'I leave to my beloved son, *An Enquiry Concerning Human Understanding.*'

'Boswell writes Hume very well, doesn't he,' says X. X puts an arm round my shoulders and looks down at the book in my lap.

We read together:

'"Well," said I, "Mr Hume, I hope to triumph over you when I meet you in a future state; and remember you are not to pretend that you was joking with all this infidelity." "No, no," said he. "But I shall have been so long there before you come that it will be nothing new." In this style of good humour and levity did I conduct the conversation. Perhaps it was wrong on so awful a subject. But as nobody was present, I thought it could have no bad effect. I however felt a degree of horror, mixed with a sort of wild, strange, hurrying recollection of my excellent mother's pious instructions, of Dr Johnson's noble lessons, and of my religious sentiments and affections through the course of my life. I was like a man in sudden danger eagerly seeking his defensive arms; and I could not but be assailed by momentary doubts while I had actually before me a man of such strong abilities and extensive inquiry dying in the persuasion of being annihilated. But I maintained my faith.'

'Oh ho!' says X. '*La mort de l'auteur c'est la naissance du lecteur.* Happy birthday Bozzy.'

'The author really is like God,' say I. 'Dead? Not dead? Opinion is divided. The Barthesian texts, meanwhile, are like the witty, iconoclastic works of Hume and Voltaire. You remember, in "*La mort de l'auteur*"? Refusing to assign a single sense to a text releases activity which is "*contre-théologique, proprement révolutionnaire, car refuser d'arrêter le sens, c'est finalement refuser Dieu et ses hypostases, la raison, la science, la loi.*" Boswell would have gone to the deathbed of Barthes.'

'The author can't die yet,' says X. '*S'il n'y avait pas d'auteur, il aurait fallu l'inventer*—capitalism requires the existence of someone to pick up the cheque.'

'I know what Barthes would have said to Boswell,' say I. '*On n'a donc rien écrit?'* I am proud of the '*on*', and wait for applause. Then it occurs to me that this is cheating. I have wilfully revived the author, or rather '*l'auteur*', constructing 'characteristic' remarks to be uttered by the collector of royalties in extremis. I could have said this at dinner. X will have something to say about it.

'Oh, you!' says X. X kisses me. 'Let's go upstairs,' says X.

There is a text which I could insert at this point which begins 'I'm not in the mood,' but the reader who has had occasion to consult it will know that, though open to many variations, there is one form which is, as Voltaire would say, *potius optandum quam probandum*, and that is the one which runs 'I'm not in the mood,' 'Oh, OK.' My own experience has shown this to be a text particularly susceptible to discursive and recursive operations, one which circles back on itself through several iterations and recapitulations, one which ends pretty invariably in 'Oh, OK,' but only about half the time as the contribution of my co-scripteur. I think for a moment about giving the thing a whirl, but finally settle on the curtailed version which leaves out 'I'm not in the mood' and goes directly to 'Oh, OK.' X and I go upstairs.

X and I sit on the bed. The subtext is suddenly too much with us, and it is clear it will soon push us into what is not spoken. X begins to move oddly: a hand traverses space but makes no gesture. X's movements, my movements must become the thing meant; X cannot approach this. The words have slipped away, the distance between signifier and signified is no doubt not very great—but the threshold of silence is daunting. X begins to talk about construction and deconstruction of gender, and succeeds again in 'placing a hand on my knee.' 'What is woman?' says X. 'Is this the mark of woman?' X puts a hand on my breast, cannily pursuing sous-texte sous prétexte.

X talks about clothes, which gesture at the difference they conceal. Or don't. X begins to undress. Each signifier, says X, signifies a further signifier. Each difference is meant and meaning. Difference gestures beyond itself. I begin to undress. X is talking very fast while unfastening all fastenings: buttons fly from holes, zips unzip, clothes fly from skin to the floor. My clothes fall to my feet. And X, who has been taking this road very fast, goes into a skid on the slippage of meaning and smashes up against silence. It is as if we have accidentally removed, with our clothes, all signs of desire and desirability, as if we have sloughed off tits cunt prick with bra skirt trousers and find ourselves, stripped of language, indifferent featherless bipeds, trying to put it all back—but we are to each other as pale and lumpish and uninteresting as Cranach's Adam and Eve. We catch each other's eyes, after all we always understand each other.

'Blue, not-blue,' say I.

X shows a flicker of interest at the Edenic language: his cock lifts its head.

'Blue and not-blue,' he replies. He thinks a moment. He holds up crossed fingers. '*Bleu*,' he says grinning. He pulls me over onto the bed, and starts kissing my breast.

We plunge at last into silence. No. Silenced, beneath X, my text goes sous-texte and presents the question: is it then the physical which makes sense of my story? Is it here that you find the array of possible meanings contracted—does this compel you to take things a certain way? Must X be a man? It seems inescapable to me.

It is as if I am lying on the bottom of a lake looking up through clear water at the sky: I see ripples across the surface at the meeting of water and air. I wonder how this looks to X. X sees, perhaps, a single body of water across which Hume, the scratch wig, that pleasing notion immortality skim and skitter like watermen.

I close my eyes. I see a vast slate-coloured ocean with an immense and wrinkled skin.

I think of one of the *fragments d'un discours amoureux*. 'This cannot go on.' I think: 'This could go on all night.'

I open my eyes. X rolls over on his back. He begins to sing softly:

'Well it ainno use ta sit an wonder hwhy babe, iffen you dont know by now. An it ainno use ta sit an wonder hwhy babe. It'll never do somehow.' X likes songs that hug the vernacular. He dwells on whatever is most untranslatable to pen and paper, whatever written language can only hint at, what written language must be distorted even to acknowledge: hoarseness—nasality—drawing out of syllables—chromatic scales through the diphthongs. X does not, of course, admit that anything could be irredeemably unwritable, his position is that all these marks of the spoken are repeatable and therefore written. But X cannot sing and state his position at the same time. Singing, X indulges in illicit joys—he will restate the position after the song.

'Well it ainno use in turnin on yer light babe. The light i—never knowed. An it ainno use in turnin on yer light babe. i'm on the dark side of the road.' X catches my eye. 'Well i wish there was sumpn you would—do er say—Ta tryen make me change m'minden stay—We never did teuu much talkin anyway—But don think twice its all right.'

X likes songs that gesture at inarticulacy. He is drawn to the poignancy of a world in which the unspoken is two-thirds of the iceberg. He is drawn to lovers who take things for granted. There are lovers, says the song, who do not include in their writing of *la situation amoureuse* the texts which play around the theme 'I'm not in the mood'—that must pare down discourse quite considerably. I myself am strangely drawn to a form of closure which leaves things so largely unsaid. X and I face a very long and wearisome collaboration on the end of the affair. Having written so much it seems we must continue: language squeezes an author like an orange. X and I are not in a position to walk away; we can part but not leave. Face to face some things are impossible to say. It'll never do somehow.

I think of telling X that we think too much alike. I imagine writing down a song and handing it to X in a note:

> You say either and I say either
> You say neither and I say neither
> Either Either Neither Neither
> Let's call the whole thing off.

> You say tomato and I say tomato
> You say potato and I say potato
> Tomato Tomato Potato Potato
> Let's call the whole thing off.

•

I am in the common room looking through the paper. x is reading a book in a dark blue cloth binding. I stand by x's shoulder, the *TLS* in my hand, and look down at the page. In a frame which consists of the angle of x's neck and shoulder, x's right forearm, x's left knee, I read:

In the Euclidean space R_n the Cauchy-Bunyakovsky inequality has the form

$$\left| \sum_{j=1}^{n} \xi_j \eta_j \right| \leq \sqrt{\sum_{j=1}^{n} \xi_j^2} \sqrt{\sum_{j=1}^{n} \eta_j}$$

it holds for any pair of vectors x = $(\xi_1 \dots \xi_n)$, y= $(\eta_1 \dots \eta_n)$, or what is the same thing, for any two systems of real numbers $\xi_1, \xi_2 \dots \xi_n$ and $\eta_1, \eta_2 \dots \eta_n$ (this inequality was discovered by Cauchy in 1821).

The frame is very simple: x's checked flannel shirt, with an open neck and short sleeve, has a Wittgensteinian innocence. The dark blue trousers are just trousers. The arm is long and bony. I am looking at the score of the music of the spheres. I gaze at this silent material for some time. The harmonies I see represented remain perfectly inaudible to me, but I see from the repose and concentration of x that x can hear them.

I have mastered subjects and failed to love them. I have looked at the sun and not been blinded; I have dimmed the sun. I will be a lover of the moon.

I lie on a bed with x. It is covered with a spread of purple chenille. The room is filled with humble objects lent dignity by the light of the moon: an electric kettle which does not switch off automatically; a mug with a picture of Miss Piggy; a box of Brooke PG Tips, a jar of coffee powder; a packet of My Mum's digestives; a skimpy blue and red striped towel thrown over a chair; a shiny orange anorak.

On the desk are a pad of graph paper, four or five medium point blue Bic biros, two or three stubby pencils, a calculator. Ranged along the back against the wall are books: *Diophantine Inequalities*, I read on a spine. *Bauer Trees of Sporadic Groups. Amenable Banach Algebras. Singular Perturbation Theory*. I suppose that these books map out truth, or at any rate truths. I believe that mathematical truths are eternal, or rather timeless; but it is comforting rather than not to have so many of these truths allied to names and dates. I have not forgotten that the Cauchy-Bunyakovsky inequality was discovered by Cauchy in 1821! x has thrown a few library books on a chair by the door: *Volterra Integrodifferential Equations in Banach Spaces and Applications. The Penrose Transform. Classical Fourier Transforms, Automorphic Forms, Shimura Varieties, and L-functions*. These names commemorate persons who heard, wrote down snatches of the piece. I am happy for them. At the same time it is sheer accident that one rather than another happened to do so—x sometimes tells me stories of simultaneous discovery. x can't see why these delight me. Sometimes I ask x 'Who was Banach?' 'What about Shimura?' 'Just who was Penrose, anyway?' just for the pleasure of hearing x's confessions of ignorance, or professions of knowledge—the answer, when x has one, is always of the form 'A was someone who discovered that B.'

X, who had views on everything, would not have stood for it. What was his line? 'The truth is that counting has proved to pay.' 'It can't be said of the series of natural numbers that it is true, but: that it is usable, and, above all, it is used.' This sounds familiar—I'm sure I remember X quoting it—but whether pro or con I can't recall. Certainly mathematics were not to have the privilege of referential semantics, but the ins and outs of the arguments for levelling escape me now. I look at the face of x, calmly intent upon a book: the light must come from somewhere.

x sometimes has a book propped open against a knee. I look over x's shoulder at *Probability Approximations via the Poisson Clumping Heuristic*; my eyes wander restfully across a page of Greek letters and brackets. x holds, sometimes, a small spiral pad, one of the blue Bic biros, from time to time x scrawls a note, pursues a line of thought in strings of symbols which modulate down the page. x's wrist lies along the edge of the pad. I see the articulation of the joint, thin delicate bones jut out beneath thin pale freckled skin; x's large knuckles clamp round the pen, bitten fingers press into the palm. How close they look! I am seeing the moon through a telescope. It is not the smooth flat surface you imagine, seeing that disc suspended in the sky; but there is a kind of wonder in seeing the rocky cratered plain which nevertheless disperses light—in seeing how, even at closer range, the line between black and brilliant white is absolute.

I put my arm around x. x's forehead is very high and pale, the skin stretched tight over the sleek pure curve of the skull. I lay my forehead against it and close my eyes. I do not strain my ears to pierce the silence; I know that within that bone and blood, a few centimetres away, plays the music of the spheres.

OXFORD, 1985

The French Style of Mlle Matsumoto

He was a pianist. He was born on the island of Shikoku, where his father had some kind of post in the administration of the prefecture of Tokushima. His mother was from Tokyo. When she married his father she had her piano brought down on the ferry to her new home. He was taught from the age of two by his mother, and from the age of eight by a woman who had studied in Paris with Koslowski until the mid-40s, when she had cut short a promising career to keep house for her widowed father.

Koslowski had said

Of all my pupils the one who showed the finest sensibility in the interpretation of Chopin was Mlle Matsumoto. To praise her technique is to say nothing. The simplicity and ease with which she executed even the most difficult passages, the absence of any kind of affectation or showmanship in pieces where it is too common to see talent on display, while the pianist plays the virtuoso, all this gave one some notion of the style of performance favored by the composer himself. We know for example on the authority of de Bertha that Chopin obtained his effects by methods very different from those of today, relying not on brute force but on gradations achieved through an infinite extension of the *piano*. This was to have the nuances, the expressive shading of the human voice or of that instrument which comes closest to the voice, the violin. His masters were a Paganini, a Bellini, a Catalani. What was remarkable was Mlle Matsumoto's ability to realize the impossible, to transform a percussive instrument into one which had the fluidity of the voice.

Her retirement has robbed music of a precious ornament but it is impossible to regret it, for it springs from the very thing which made her playing incomparable—I refer to the complete absence of self...

This was not the opinion of the pupil of Koslowski's who achieved the greatest renown. He did not hesitate to express his views on the Automaton in the most intemperate language.

Morhange said later

All sorts of contemptible things were done during the War and even later, and they did not stop at the door of the Conservatoire. One of these was old Koslowski's retention of Mlle Matsumoto, undoubtedly to curry favor with the Nazis, while at the same time washing his hands of anyone with any sort of Jewish connection—

Elle avait du talent, oui, mais elle jouait d'une façon tout à fait machinale, there was a tiresome perfection about her performance—

Koslowski said later that he had been obliged to cut back on his teaching and that M. Morhange had always shown himself so absolutely indifferent, if not positively hostile, to all suggestions on his own part that he had not supposed it would be a hardship to the young man to be deprived of them.

Morhange said that after the War it was of course even more necessary for him to present his actions under the guise of a simple pedagogical decision, one could naturally not admit that anyone had been excluded on account of the Semitic factor, it was therefore necessary to insist on the lack of talent, on aesthetic defects, which by coincidence happened to be found in Jewish persons.

The virtues of the French style were usually said to be clearness of phrasing, richness of shading, a predominance of the legato element, a strict avoidance of tempo rubato. While it was not true that Morhange had the vices which were the opposite of those virtues, his attack on the keyboard was something very different. The massive shoulders hulked over the keys; fingers like cigars grabbed at chords like bunches of bananas.

Morhange had extraordinarily long arms and a powerful upper body which he had developed further through prolonged exercise on a set of rings and bars at the local gymnasium. He was known to his fellow students as the Gorilla. One of them said later that one of the strangest sights he had ever seen was that of the Gorilla going through his daily gymnastics: he had a strong, though not particularly attractive, voice with a huge range, and as he went through the various contortions of the ring or the bar he would sing phrases from Alkan's *Funeral March for a Dead Parrot*. Oddest of all, he said, was the way no one else in the room took the slightest notice, for it was apparently by now commonplace. Above his head a figure hurtled through the air—

As-tu déjeuné, Jacquo?

The figure hurtled back—

Eh de quoi?

& back again, on a cascade of notes of inexpressible pathos:

Ah! Ah! Ah! Ah! Ah!

As-tu déjeuné?
As-tu déjeuné?
As-tu déjeuné?
As-tu déjeuné?
As-tu déjeuné, Jacquo?

Eh de quoi?
Eh de quoi?
Ah!

He was asked later whether he found it difficult to take on a pupil who had been trained by someone whom he had regarded with undisguised contempt.

—Contempt?

—You spoke of the pianism of the Machine Age—

—I said that?

—Yes.

—You play the violin?

—No?

—The violoncelle?

—Unfortunately not.

—The piano is quite a clumsy instrument by comparison and yet if I had to play a little phrase of three or four notes it would be easy to play it fifty or sixty different ways, words are much more clumsy still. I don't say that I did not say what you said I said a minute ago, or even that it wasn't my opinion years ago, but words bother me. I think that's why when I talk I often say stupid or banal or offensive things, & then people quote you and say Well why did you say this or But you said that or But don't you think this—& I want to say, well I had to say some words. I don't go around with a lot of words in my head, most of the time there is something going on my head but it's a piece of music, the minute I wake up I might lie in bed for an hour or two just listening to something in my head and if I think of different ways it might be played I don't even have the words What if I played it like this? in my head, I just hear it one way and then another and then another—if someone asks me a question I want to play some little phrase, I want to say, the way I played that piece, that's what I really mean—

—What about the Affaire Jacquo?

—What about it?

—Were you surprised by the outrage?

—Oh, surprised—

The Gorilla said there was nothing much to say, but then he said What you must understand is that I was bitterest about Koslowski before the truth about the camps was known, once that was known—

What I mean is that Koslowski was a stupid old man, he existed in a world bounded by the solfège and prizes and three or four posts to which he might rise, a ribbon that might be put on his chest. He considered Jewishness in a pupil an obstacle to advancement. What I mean is that I spent two years as a waiter in Marseille as a result of that blockhead, but once the truth was known I could not accuse the Fossil of anti-Semitism without hyperbole—

The thing you have to remember is that immediately after the War people didn't know about the camps. It was only later on that the facts started to come out. The thing you have to remember is that I never read the papers, so at first I just heard chance comments here and there, and then I did buy a paper and read an article which described some of those things for the first time—

Anyway I read this article and— You know that little C minor prelude of Chopin, you know DUM. DUM. DUM. de DUM, it's like a little funeral march, it establishes the minor key in the first chord and sometimes it's fortissimo and sometimes pianissimo and it comes and goes, it's a little funeral march— Anyway the article presented certain details and all of a sudden this little funeral march presented itself with its minor key and its fortissimo and its pianissimo as if to say, Well, here I am, something suitable to mark the occasion—well the whole idea of major and minor keys loud and soft fast and slow comprising suitability seemed fatuous—other grand sombre pieces came to my mind as if to say Of course that little prelude won't do you want something bigger you want some more dissonances you want something very simple you want something tragic and it was stupid.

It was the same when I went to practice, no matter what I did everything seemed stupid, I mean the things one tries to bring out in a passage seemed stupid, the trajectory of a piece seemed stupid, it's one thing to work on technical difficulties everyone does that from time to time but sooner or later you've got to bring the piece to life & now they were just wooden puppets with wooden arms gesturing on a string—

I thought, That's it, I'll never be able to play again, & I was

135

trying to think of some job, & meanwhile if you can believe it my parents were urging me to get married—

Anyway I really didn't know what to do with myself. Before, I would go to the gymnasium for a couple of hours to improve my upper body strength and then I would go and practice for about eight hours or maybe more if it was going really well or if there was some problem, all of a sudden there was this big hole in the day. I was still going to the gymnasium just to have something to do, but the rest of the time there was just nothing. Then suddenly I had an idea. I thought, *I* know, I'll read a *book*.

When I was at school my teachers used to get mad at me because I never did any work, & later the Fossil used to throw up his hands in horror because I'd never read Racine or Balzac or anyone like that, he'd start talking about the musician as homme cultivé— I used to say to him, If you would like me to compose an opera based on the *Phèdre* of M. Racine I shall be happy to examine the work in question, otherwise I have not the slightest desire to read this, I have no doubt, excellent play. This used to drive the Fossil insane. He would trot out some remark about oeuvre séminale de la littérature française, frankly it was amusing to see him boil up, well there was an element of truth in it but it was also the fact that I simply could not read more than a page—no, a sentence—without some piece of music coming into my head. I really did try to read *Phèdre* once & I got as far as Depuis plus de six mois éloigné de mon père, j'ignore le destin d'une tête si chère, & then all of a sudden this string quintet of Mozart's that I had heard the night before came into my head & half an hour later it finished & I was still looking at Depuis plus de six mois éloigné de mon père, j'ignore le destin d'une tête si chère. This always happened whenever I tried to read something so I never read anything, but now it was pretty quiet in my head.

Well, I had a lot of books left over from school, & at first I thought I would read *Phèdre* by Racine, anyway I looked at my little bookshelf & I had a little Greek text of Thucydide which like all my books had been cut on the first two pages. It was still pretty quiet in my head so I started to read, & there was a preface by Raymond Levecque, maybe you know this, this author had two ways of writing, one quite plain and the other barbarous & scarcely grammatical, there's a section of Book 3 about a civil war at Cercyre, & apparently it's quite famous though I'd never heard of it, it's about how all the words change when people do something atrocious, so they would call a bad thing by a good name and a good thing by a bad name, & in trying to express this he writes this very contorted Greek.

I thought, This sounds interesting, I'll look at that. But it was very bizarre, you know, it had a translation on the facing page and they had put it into civilized grammatical French. You could see what it was supposed to mean right away. But in the Greek most of the time you couldn't really see, you had to try to make it mean something because the words crammed so much in or left so much out or maybe just barely touched what the dictionary said they meant and just barely touched the grammar and just. I thought that this author had tried to let unspeakable things do something to the language and then M. Levecque had tidied it up again. I looked at this polite little sentence & sat crying on the bed—

—All the same, the *Funeral March for a Dead Parrot*
—No, not at all, that's precisely
—But many people
—Exactly
—But surely
—On the contrary

For the next thirty years Morhange was one of the most celebrated pianists in the world.

In 1975 he retired to Japan, & by coincidence took a house on the very island, in the very town where Mlle Matsumoto lived.

—Why Japan?

—Japan had fascinated me for a long time—the prints of Utamaro and Hokusai and Hiroshige—those remarkable little poems, the haiku—it is an art of subtraction, an art with a horror of the extraneous, but it's not so much that it has a horror of the extraneous as that it avoids histrionics, Western art gives the impression by contrast of being saturated with sincerity—

It was pointed out that his greatest triumphs had been with Rachmaninov, Tchaikovsky—

—Yes, exactly, it's precisely for that reason that Japanese art really struck me. As a young man I had nothing but contempt for the Fossil, an old man who in the first place understood nothing of the works he pretended to teach, who was flattered by the deference he received from Mlle Matsumoto, something which a Japanese—and a young girl at that—accords so readily to a teacher. What I did not see at the time was that there was something genuine in her performance—

What happened you see was that, when I had spent many years in America, someone happened to play me a recording of Mlle Matsumoto playing Chopin's fourth Ballade. This was the very piece with which I had won the Prix d'Orphée. I was astonished by a performance which seemed to anticipate so much of the last twenty years, & in justice to myself I listened to the recording I myself had made at that time. I was filled with contempt. If Delacroix could have played the piano, this theatrical display is precisely what he would have produced—

Hearing Mlle Matsumoto's recording I now saw the quality I had been unable to see before, that she had escaped the fatal plunge into egotism which the idiocy of the Fossil forced upon all his pupils of any talent, & had extracted something better from within herself—

138

I finished my tour—I went to Tokyo—c'était affreux—I thought that the true Japan was elsewhere—I crossed the sea to Shikoku, an island with 88 Buddhist shrines—I had my Steinway brought from Paris, as well as an old pedalier which I had managed to pick up—

I discovered that it was here that Mlle Matsumoto still lived. I remembered my behavior & could not approach her.

For eight years I lived in this town without meeting her. I knew where she lived, for once walking I heard the fourth Ballade & there could not have been two to play it in such a place. Thereafter I avoided the street.

One day after walking in the country I came back & walked down her street—I heard the opening bars of Chopin's fourth Ballade in F minor. More than ever was I conscious that I had wronged her—I felt that I must apologize—in agony I walked up and down outside the door, waiting for her to finish—double octaves in the bass melted into the air in a legato of the most perfect unhurried simplicity—I saw suddenly an insuperable difficulty. It is regarded in Japan as a common politeness to take off the shoes on entering a house—but I have always been careless of clothes, I remembered suddenly that that morning I had not been able to find any socks, that I had put on a blue and a red, each with a large hole at the big toe—I could not appear to Mlle Matsumoto like this. Like a madman I ran through the streets of Tokushima, I found a shop, I bought a pair of socks, in my mind I heard the Ballade approaching the arpeggiated chords before the end, I flung down a few yen & ran off, I darted into the precincts of a nearby shrine—no one in sight—I took off my shoes & the old socks, bundled the latter into a pocket, put on the new, put on my shoes, dashed to the house of Mlle Matsumoto. She had come to the moment of stillness before the final explosion. It came to an end—gathering my courage I knocked—she came to the door—I must speak to you, I said, you must allow me to apologize—she gestured for me to enter—I removed my shoes & followed her—we entered the room with the piano—I stood before her, every word of Japanese left my head, I poured forth my reflections of a decade & when I paused she said

Vous êtes très aimable, M. Morhange, mais ce n'est point à moi que vous devez addresser vos louanges,

& she gestured toward the piano.

C'est mon élève que vous venez d'entendre,

& she introduced me to a twelve-year-old boy who bowed without speaking.

I stammered something, bowed & left—just after me the boy burst from the house & ran down the street—& now Chopin's fourth Ballade came again from the house—but I could not go back.

The following week I received a note from Mlle Matsumoto asking me to take on Murakami as a pupil.

Stolen Luck

Keith was not the songwriter. Darren and Stewart wrote the songs. Keith hit things, some of which were drums. He came in one day with a song and nobody wanted to play it.

The song was the least of their problems. They had signed with a label, so their music was used in adverts and that, it brought in some dosh, they were shameless rock sluts because the fans down-loaded the songs for free. Slutdom was not the issue. The issue was that the contract would not let them do independent gigs.

Keith had had an argument with them because the Arctic Monkeys, look at the fucking Arctic Monkeys, why the fuck can't we do what the fucking Arctic Monkeys, this being the capacity for inarticulate rage which had made him a drummer in the first

And Darren and Stewart, being songwriters, had talked and talked and talked and talked to the point that there were signatures on the contract.

Then the inconceivable had happened which is that Thom Yorke sent an e-mail inviting them to do a gig. Keith said they should just do it, fuck the fucking contract but Darren and Stewart

So then Keith was very quiet.

Never a good sign.

Given Keith's known propensity to hit things other than drums.

So Darren said they would record the song.

Keith tried to explain his concept and Darren and Stewart kept arsing about and then Sean the keyboardist sussed that it was an arsing about session and then Keith put down his sticks.

Darren, Stewart and Sean sussed that the beat was gone.

Keith, says Darren. What the fuck.

Keith disengaged from the scaffolding of things that could be hit that made noise. He stood up.

He walked across the floor while Darren, Stewart and Sean varied the theme of What the fuck. He took the mic from Darren.

In addition to not being a songwriter Keith was not a singer. He dragged the lyrics of the song over reluctant vocal cords and spat them into the mic.

Fucking great man said Darren who did not want another guitar percussioned to subatomic particles against wall, floor, chair, his head. Yeah fucking great said Stewart who had also lost 3 guitars and Sean hastened to protect his keyboard from berserk drummer syndrome, Fucking great, insane, totally fucking crazy man

Keith handed the mic back to Darren. He turned and walked out the door.

The studio was in Limehouse. He walked west. His legs would not let him get on a bus.

At Leicester Square the crowd, wasn't there a director who gave every person in a crowd scene a thing to do? Sometimes the world is too convincing, as if someone spent too much time on it. Individualising the robots. He stopped at a corner.

On the pavement was this, like, guy with a sign beside him, CRAZY NICK AND HIS MUSICAL TRAFFIC CONES. There was an orange cone on the pavement beside him and he was holding another cone to his mouth, blowing into it. To the music of My Way.

pa PA, pa PA pa PA, pa PA pa PA, pa PA pa PA pa
pa PA, pa PA pa PA, pa PA pa PA, pa PA pa PA pa

People were dropping money in the cone. One woman, she put a ten pound note in the fucking cone.

PA PA PA pa PA
pa PA pa PA
PA PA PA PA PA

He stood on the pavement.

pa pa
pa pa pa pa
pa pa pa——PAAAAAA PA

Like, fuck. A kid put 10p in the cone. The music was shite but here was this luckless tosser turning ostensibly irredeemable shite into gold with a simple traffic cone. Single-handedly handling his own PR and marketing and sales and distribution. Say Thom Yorke comes upon the scene, says Hey, Crazy Nick, great act, OK if I join you, and Thom Yorke picks up the other traffic cone and does an impromptu gig with Crazy Nick—

Crazy Nick can say Yes, he can say Fuck off Radiohead wanker scum. Total artistic control.

He stood watching Crazy Nick for about 3 hours because

He walked east.

Marc was on the late shift at the News of the World. He wore a suit because hacks must dig for dirt in a suit. A call came in that a celeb was being a wanker in a pub, if swift action was taken photographic evidence might be shared with the British public, and Marc was the man for the job.

The celeb was Kyle Vaughan. He had a part in a soap. He stood by the bar with a rolled-up copy of the Big Issue, blowing My Way out of the orifice. Poop POOP poop POOP poop POOP poop POOP poop POOP poop POOP poop poop poop.

Not much value in it as a pic.

What I'm saying is, they're not doing enough to TRAIN, expatiated the celeb. Like, show some initiative, mate. You see them selling the Big Toilet Tissue and you want to say look, I have enough problems without constipating my brain with this crap, do something funny for a change, add value to the product

Marc: So you'd, like,

Like today I saw this bloke at Leicester Square, Crazy Nick and His Musical Traffic Cones, he's playing My Way on a traffic cone, I thought, you know, this just goes to show how fucking useless the Big Issue is, anyone with a little imagination can do more with a couple of fucking traffic cones

So you, did you give him some money, then? asked Marc.

Yeh. I gave him a quid. Which is what I'm saying.

Poop POOP poop POOP poop POOP poop POOP poop POOP poop POOP poop poop poop.

But maybe, maybe everyone can't be that innovative, do you think there's enough funny things that homeless people can do? Could you, like, do you have any ideas?

Yeh. Sure. Like. Like. Say you say to people, I am going to take my trousers off. If you pay me I will put them back on.

Yeh, maybe, said Marc, but see, maybe that's quite embarrassing, taking off your trousers in front of a lot of strangers, I mean, you wouldn't want to do it

Poop POOP poop POOP poop POOP poop POOP poop POOP poop POOP poop poop poop.

That's where you're wrong, mate. Because it's not about being a humung being it's about putting on a performance

Yeh but I don't see you doing it, easy to say, said Marc

144

And then it all happens very fast, the celeb is waving his Diesel jeans around his head and Marc is snapping pix and the celeb is shouting Wanker and Marc is heading for the door and the celeb is struggling to get into his Diesel jeans and Marc is in the street running

and he ducks into a doorway three swift corners down

and he gets out his phone and sends pix and they are dead chuffed, well done mate, they say

and he walks under the cold sky on wet tarmac on which the bones of chickens and crumbs of fried batter mingle with dog turds, shiny crisp packets, a flattened satsuma, he steps into the Oranges & Lemons & at the pinball machine is Keith O'Connor.

Marc orders a pint of Guinness. O'Connor is dancing with the pinball machine, pulling knobs, slapping the glass, leaning into it, pulling away. Marc sits on a plump leather bench. It's quiet.

The door opens. A bloke in a Tommy Hilfiger sweatshirt and Diesel jeans, bald, red face, goes to the bar, orders a Peroni, goes through swinging doors to a room behind the bar.

You all right, Tel.

Yeh. Yeh.

No offence mate but you look like shit.

Yeh. Well, me missus kicked me out.

Fuck.

Yeh— See, I was sitting at the end of the bar and this old geezer is talking to this girl and I say the word *cunt*. Not loud, like, but I do say it, but in a private conversation. So he hears me, and this is partly generational, he takes offence because his girl is there. So he says What did you say? So I don't want to make an issue of it, so I say All right, Stan, leave it, but he won't leave it alone, he says What did you say, so at this point I go over not meaning to do any serious damage but just to, you know, give him a little tap, but I misjudged the situation and broke his jaw.

Fuck.

Yeh. Yeh. This old geezer, and you know I would not normally hit someone that age Derek but he gave me no option, but then me missus says, You're not coming home.

Fuck.

Yeh.

Well, you can stay at mine or you can stay here. Frank and his lot are coming over after unloading, usual game.

It's been a long day.

The pinball machine is silent. Keith feeds it more coins. Marc occupies his suit.

Derek: In the north *cunt* is still an offensive word. You say that around somebody's girlfriend and he will exterminate you. In the south you hear it all over the place, people say Stop cunting me about, this sort of thing.

Tel: I'm all cunted out. I've heard that.

Derek: So stop cunting me about, you cunt, are you in or out.

Tel: Yeh all right then

Derek: You know what they say Tel, unlucky in love, this could just be your lucky night

Tel: Yeh. Yeh.

Teetleep Teetleep Teetleep Peep!

Teetleep Teetleep Teetleep Peep!

Beep! Beep!

Bebeep Beep Beep, Beep Beep Beep

Sorry, Tel, I think this is Frank—Frank, what the fuck, mate—yeh, yeh, sorry to hear that, Tel's here, yeh his missus was aggravated by an assault of Colonel Blimp or what have you so looks like Tel will be selling the Big Issue or something, yeh, help the homeless, so we on for tonight.

The pinball machine is silent. Marc is silent, nursing his foamy Guinness. Banter is tossed nonchalantly into the plastic mouthpiece, it is snatched from the air to burst forth at a distant earpiece, fresh banter pours into the waiting ear, it seems two of Frank's lot have been taken into custody, so if it's just the four of them including Tel maybe that is not enough to make it worthwhile, names of possible substitutes are proposed and rejected amid banter

Sorry, hold on Frank, yeh what is it?

Keith is standing at the bar. He wears a black t-shirt with a skeleton. His eyes are thickly mascaraed. There is glitter on his cheeks.

He says: You having a poker game?

Derek: We're talking about a friendly game among friends, mate.

Keith: This is how much money I have.

He takes a wallet from his back pocket and opens it, showing a thick soft pad of notes. This being the level of social savoir faire which led to Keith being a drummer in the

Derek: Yeh, well

Goes back on the phone with Frank.

Dunno, he says, bloke here might be up for it but I dunno, Frank, five, snot much of a game

But Marc is on his feet. This is KEITH O'CONNOR, drummer of the MISSING LYNX—

Marc is not into the pathos of semiotically enhanced footwear, is it a riposte to dualism that the intestines propel partially digested chicken tikka masala into the circumambient air when the eyes pass over the cover of a pb by Tony Parsons? What does it tell us of the human condition if the mind, pursuant to the expulsion of comestibles, explores the opposition between tearjerking & dickjerking—and yet somehow separate from the crap that now is Parsons is the history, the hack cavorting w/ Johnny Rotten, this is a chance that will never

Words come to the plausible mouth.

I can play a bit, he says.

They are looking at the Suit, he should introduce the Suit separately, the estate of Lord Carnarvon had given his wardrobe to the

Notting Hill Trust and now a garment that the body of a British aristocrat had worn to the House of Lords in 1953 (where it had excited no comment) had been handed into the keeping of a pleb for twenty quid to walk the world in low company.

And, like, Gerry! Maybe Gerry would like to play.

A sign above the door states that Gerald O'Hanlon is the proprietor licenced to sell intoxicating beverages.

Derek says: Don't be daft, Gerry's been up since 6 am, last thing he wants is

Gerry says: You only live once.

He says: Look, Tel should not be on his own.

Marc scents: The money in the wallet, this is the thing they won't mention.

So it happens. Frank and the fortuitously uncustodised Maury are in their midst, Gerry locks up, there are seven men in a room behind swinging doors back of the bar.

They're playing Texas Hold 'em because that's what they've seen on TV.

For those who have not seen the game on TV: it's a doddle. Each player is dealt two cards. There's a round of betting. Three cards are dealt down the middle—the flop. A round of betting. A card is dealt—the turn. Another round of betting. A last card is dealt—the river. A final round of betting. Each player can combine any three of the cards on the table with the two in his hand to make up a 'poker hand'; the one with the best hand wins.

Marc has £51.63. The usual suspects are all buying chips for a friendly couple of hundred quid, which Marc reckons is to encourage Keith to do the same. Keith does buy in for a couple of hundred, which means Marc has to buy in for fifty quid. He does not expect to win; if he can walk away without losing more than five quid he'll count himself lucky. He's just trying to remember the ranking of hands as seen on TV.

Pair, two pair, three of a kind, Straight is five cards in numerical order. Flush is five cards of same suit, Flush beats a straight? Straight beats a flush? Full house is pair plus three of a kind. Four of a kind. Straight flush does what it says on the tin.

How many poker hands do you want to hear about?

You need to know about 3.

Marc started out with £50. On the third hand he picks up A K of spades. He bets 50p. Maury raises him £1. Frank sees the £1.50 and raises £1.50. Gerry sees the £3 and raises £3. Derek calls. Keith folds. Tel calls.

Marc thinks: Shit.

He calls.

Maury calls. Frank calls. The flop is King of diamonds Jack of diamonds 8 of spades. Marc checks. Maury bets £5. Frank folds. Gerry and Derek call.

Marc thinks: Shit.

He calls.

The turn is the 10 of spades. Marc bets £10. Maury calls. Gerry folds. Derek calls. The river is the Jack of spades. Marc bets £2. Maury raises him £10. Marc calls. Maury has Ace of diamonds Queen of diamonds. Marc wins £113.50.

It is obvious to everyone that Marc does not know what the fuck he is doing. Marc plays cautiously for the next 20 hands or so while Keith loses all his chips and buys in for another £300. There is much face-to-face banter.

Marc has inched his way up to £150. He would like to leave but he sits folding hand after hand. He picks up 8 9 of clubs. He is the big blind. He is in for 50p. Maury, Frank, Gerry, Tel and Keith stay in. The flop goes down and it is 10 7 of clubs J of spades.

Marc bets £2.

Maury raises £2. Frank, Gerry and Tel call. Keith raises £20. Marc thinks: Shit.

He has seen the hands Keith has been betting on. He calls.

Maury, Frank, Gerry and Tel have seen the hands Keith has been betting on. They call. The turn is the 6 of clubs. Marc bets £5. Maury calls. Frank raises £10. Gerry folds. Tel calls. Keith raises £20. Marc calls. Maury folds. Frank calls. Tel folds.

The river goes down and it is the 9 of diamonds. Marc bets £10. Frank raises £20. Keith calls. Marc calls.

Frank has A K clubs. Keith has K Q of hearts.

Put Frank's hand with the board and you get A K 10 7 6 clubs. A flush. Which beats Keith's K Q (hearts) plus J (spades) 10 (clubs) 9 (diamonds). A straight.

After 3 hours Marc is totally confident that a flush beats a straight. So Keith is fucked. And under normal circumstances Frank's flush to the Ace would beat Marc's flush to the 10. But Marc, he checks again, yeah, he definitely has 10 9 8 7 6 of clubs, which is a straight flush. So they are BOTH well and truly fucked by the King of the Hacks.

He thinks.

He hesitates to rake in the chips which he thinks are now rightfully his. There may be some arcane fact of poker lore such that if he shows he thinks he won he will look like a twat.

Derek says: I feel your pain, Frank.

Fucking A!!!!!!!!!!!!!!!!!!!!!!!

As it says in the song, you don't count your money when you're sitting at the table. Basically Marc has won what is technically known as a shitload. He stacks the unexamined chips at his left.

Gerry says: I been up since 6, mates.

Tel says: You only live once, Ger.

Marc thinks: Shut. The fuck. Up. Just go to bed, you fucking wanker.

He thinks: But I don't have to

He's shivering. All he has to do is avoid fucking up and he can walk out with, like, 500 quid.

Marc does not feel he is really engaging with Keith, who seems to be in a chip-scattering bubble of solipsistic frenzy. He is not picking up anything NME-worthy. He feels like a twat in the Suit. It's also unbelievably boring. But if he can manage to survive the bollocks-withering tedium of the game he can

How many hands do you seriously want to hear about?

They play for another hour. Keith buys in for another £400. Marc tries to play unadventurously without looking like a cunt. Something in the ambience tells him he is not succeeding.

What happens.

Marc picks up 7 of diamonds 2 of clubs. He folds. Derek, Maury, Frank, Gerry, Tel and Keith stay in. The flop: A K hearts 6 spades. Derek is in for £5. Maury, Frank, Ger see him. Tel raises an unfriendly £50. Keith sees him and he is all in, which is to say that the wallet is now empty. There is an adjustment to the ambience. Marc gives it another 10 minutes before they pack it in and go home.

He can see them getting ready to fold, no point sending good money after bad, the hard faces with their pebble eyes assessing the exhaustion of the night's bounty.

Keith says: Look mate, I'll give you an IOU.

Ger says: No offence mate but cash only.

And Keith says: Look, I'm with a band. We've been signed and that. Four songs in the top 10. Missing Lynx.

Derek says: No offence mate but we would not take an IOU from Mick Jagger.

Meaning they have never fucking heard of the band.

And Marc in his 15 seconds of brain death says: Fucking fantastic band.

Keith turns to him. Maybe Marc is expecting to bond, as Tony Parsons allegedly did with Johnny Rotten and Joe Strummer and the giants of the past.

Keith says: Look, mate. I wrote a song. We recorded it today. If

I assign the copyright to you, like, you can lend me 500 quid with the song as collateral.

Which is the way even a drummer can end up thinking and talking if he has spent quality time among the suits.

And the ambience adjusts yet again. Because now there is the possibility of transferring the dosh at Marc's elbow out of the safe custody of a hack who has been checking and folding all night, into the unsafe hands of a raving percussionist.

Go on then old cock, be a sport, says Frank, and Maury says, Least you can do, seeing as you're a fan and all, and Derek says, Got a piece of paper, Ger? And Ger says, Anything to help a friend,

and suddenly Keith is writing something on a cocktail napkin and signing it and now Marc is sitting there with a cocktail napkin and Keith has many many many piles of chips.

Derek folds. The rest stay in, heartened by the influx of chips at the disposal of El Loco. The turn brings a 6 of hearts. Tel bets another unfriendly £50. Keith sees him. Frank sees him. Maury sees him. Ger folds. The last card goes down. It's the King of spades. Tel bets £50. Keith raises £50. Frank and Maury fold. Tel raises £50. Keith goes all in, moving all Marc's former chips to the center of the table. Tel sees him. Cards go down.

Keith has two Aces, making a full house.

Tel has two sixes.

Making 4 of a kind.

Keith says:
Pa PA pa PA pa PA
pa PA pa PA pa PA
pa PA pa PA pa

Unlucky in love, Tel, says Derek. Remind me never to play with you again when yer missus kicks you out.

They're standing up, stretching, grumbling, talking about next week. It's over.

Tel is a grand ahead.

Keith has an empty wallet.

Marc has an autographed cocktail napkin.

Marc and Keith stand outside the Oranges and Lemons in the resentful London dawn.

Marc feels the severed 500 quid like an amputated limb. He's holding the cocktail napkin. It feels both worthless and, like, something he shouldn't have.

He says: Look, uh, Keith, you'd better have this back, I can't keep this.

Keith says: You can then. Not to worry, I'll pay you back. Gissa phone number.

Marc says: I'll show you mine if you'll show me yours.

He wants to say: This is not actually my suit. But this would involve explaining that he is a loathsome creature of Murdoch employ, perhaps insufficient exculpation.

He says: Uh, I'm actually a freelance journalist? Any chance I could, like, interview you sometime?

Keith looks at the Suit.

Styrofoam cups are trundling down the desolation of the Commercial Road under an indifferent breeze.

He says: Look. I want you to do me a favour.

Marc says: Yeah sure

Keith: You got whatever the fuck it is you wanted. So just wank off.

Marc: But

Keith: Just fucking Wank. the Fuck. Off.

Keith O'Connor is walking away.

The Suit knows how to deal with the situation. From a pocket comes a hand holding a phone.

ZZZZZZZslik. ZZZZZZZslik.

And for the fuck of it out of the practiced mouth comes: Hey KEITH!

And Keith O'Connor turns, slik slik slik slik

And Keith shouts: Wank OFF wank OFF you fucking wanker

And he turns again and he turns into a side street and Marc thinks: You stiffed me half a grand you wanker so who's the wanker

It's pretty quiet.

He puts the phone back in the convenient outside pocket. His hand touches something soft, the paper napkin. He transfers it to the inside pocket of Carnarvon's finest.

He can't use his last £1.63 on transportation, it has to see him to the end of the month. He trudges west.

At 7 am Marc is in the Kingsway Starbucks recounting the evening's squalor to Lucy, who slips him a mega mocha latte and 3 blueberry muffins. He spends the next 5 hours rererererecounting to Claire at the Kingsway Caffé Nero, Nikki at the Holborn Pret A Manger, Eva at the Kingsway Costa Coffee, scoring much-needed provisions for the fundless month.

At noon the Evening Standard hauls in the punters with sorrowful news: KEITH O'CONNOR TRAGIC SUICIDE. He palms a discarded copy in the Shakespeare's Head and reads with shock and dismay.

But he is down to his last £1.63.

And he is on the phone to his minders at the News of the World with his scoop and they are dead chuffed, Well done mate, give us anything you got, and sure, Roger will be only too happy to reimburse the two hundred quid Marc allegedly lost in the game as a business expense, any pix, they would love to run a centre spread but they would love to have pix, well of course he has pix, what do you think? He has pix of Keith O'Connor's departing back heading down the desolation of the Commercial Road.

In this fashion did he honour Keith O'Connor's last request.

He did in fact write an in-depth analysis of the evening for NME.

Missing Lynx did in fact release the previously maligned song as a single. Which with tragic irony went straight to Number 5 in the charts and remained in the top 10 for an amazing 20 weeks.

Marc still has his cocktail napkin which still feels both worthless and like something he should not have. When the song has been at Number 5 for 6 weeks he sidles into the office of the lawyer at the Screws and brings the soft thing from the inside breast pocket of the aristocratic garment, anticipating that he will be dismissed as a twat for even contemplating the possibility that the relic of Oranges and Lemons revelry could be operational in a court of law.

Gayatri says: Crikey. Well done you!

She says: If they contest you might need witnesses, but as far as the language goes this is the business.

We can reveal that Darren and Stewart had spent many hours analysing the source of Sting's wealth, which derives not least from the fact that he is the author of record of such classics as 'Every Breath You Take', 'Roxanne', 'Message in a Bottle', and 'Every Little Thing She Does Is Magic', such that he receives a fee in the region of $.08 (as of time of writing) every time said songs get air time, years or even decades after the songs slipped off the charts never to return. Whilst the other members of Police get bugger all. The result being that Darren and Stewart had spent many hours arguing over credits for the songs of Missing Lynx, while Sean on keyboards and Keith on drums were never even conceivably going to be in a position to buy an island in the Caribbean. Such that

Keith had lost valuable time that might have been spent hitting things absorbing the Language of the Suits by osmosis. Which stood him in good stead when he needed to transfer copyright to a song on a cocktail napkin.

So yeah, needless to say Darren and Stewart were not going to take this lying down, but Marc's newfound mates at the Oranges and Lemons rallied round, and Sean the keyboardist unexpectedly refused to remember that the song had been more of a thing they had all done together than something any one person could take credit for, and Marc was quids in.

You can't always get what you want.

Pa Pa Pa PAAAAAAAAAAAA Pa.

In Which Nick Buys a Harley for 16k
Having Once Been Young

In 1970 they had their one and only legendary US tour.

The Breaks played 100 gigs in 110 days. They played their five hits the way the hits sounded on the record. They played their six other songs so they sounded like their five hits. They were in America, which was where they had all dreamed of going, except they didn't see it. They saw hotel rooms and stages and the inside of a bus.

The tour was not going well, because before they left their manager had brought out their new LP. The last time they had talked about the cover Pete had had some Op Art-like ideas and their manager had said it was interesting and now here it was.

The artwork was a rip-off of Yellow Submarine with cartoons of the lads in bell-bottoms and boots and it was called Groovin On Down. There was an unpleasant scene because Pete said he was not going to America to be associated with an album called Groovin On Down. His manager said he did not see and Pete said bitterly that they should call themselves the Berks and a bystanding American asked enlightenment and was told that a berk was the kind of person who thought it was groovy to call an album Groovin On Down. Wee Willie Wanker and His Wallies he said, and he said Well at least they can't do anything to

There was something about the way Steve's expression stayed exactly the same so smiling and friendly there was something in the way he said agreeing Exactly, it's the music the fans care about, slipping in the word 'fans'.

Pete said Well let's hear it, and there was something about the way he was too eager. He slipped the silky black disc from its sleeve and put it on the turntable.

Some of the record was old material and some was new material going in a different direction from the old material which now sounded exactly like the old material.

The three other Breaks jumped him before he could kill their manager and their manager explained that they had just made some very minor adjustments because you didn't want to disappoint your fans.

For a while it seemed that Pete would not go but someone had the bright idea of calling his father who made an uplifting speech about Shirley Temple, that little girl had more spunk in her little finger was the general tenor of the argument, look at Julie Andrews he went on to say, do you think Miss Andrews found it easy to work with a man who imagined he had mastered Cockney? These people are professionals, he explained, it's not all glamour, it's a tough life but the show must go on.

Pete hung up and relayed the comment about Shirley Temple to the rest of the band.

The Beatles had staff to do their autographing but the Breaks wouldn't do that to their fans. Every manager has to find his own way of dealing with temperament. What Steve did was he talked to the lads before the tour, he said it meant a lot to the fans to have a signed copy of the album, Pete, he said, as they all knew, he said, had a big following amongst the fans, but he knew Pete was not as happy as he had hoped with the album, he respected that, if Pete was not comfortable with signing the album he could just sign pix and Mike, Nick and Dave could sign albums on Pete's behalf but he naturally hoped that in the cold light of day Pete would see his way to doing something that would mean so much to the fans. At the end of the day they were all professionals.

Pete didn't say anything. There were four stacks of pix of the lads, and a stack of Groovin On Down. Mike, Nick and Dave each took twenty copies of Groovin On Down. Pete said Well, if it means that much to the fans, and he took twenty copies of Groovin On Down and started signing.

So Steve had the lads signing pix and LPs for a couple of hours a day before the gigs. By the second week of the tour three of the songs on the album were in the Top 10. The three hits were all from the new material that had been toned down to be more like the old material.

Steve did not expect gratitude because he was just doing his job, which was to see they did not disappoint the fans.

Luckily at the gigs the lads were not really able to replicate the sound effects Pete had been aiming at in the studio, so the three new hits sounded even more like the five old hits than they did on the record.

One day they were doing a Break-tastic group signing. Nick had to leave the room so Mike took some albums signed Mike and Dave over to Pete and when Nick came back he found he had a stack of albums signed Mike, Dave and Willy the Wanker.

It was only too clear that Pete had failed to live up to the standard of professionalism set by Miss Temple and Miss Andrews.

Steve said it wasn't for himself that he minded, it was the fans, he thought they were all professionals, but if that was the way it had to be so be it.

What it meant was that in later years any copy of Groovin On Down signed Mike Nick Dave and Pete was automatically worthless, because Pete had only ever signed the album Willy the Wanker, Wee Willie Wanker, and Shirley, and the only ones signed Pete dated from the point at which Steve had brought in a girl to sign on Pete's behalf. The Willy the Wanker albums were worth about $1,000, and a complete Willy the Wanker–Wee Willie Wanker–Shirley set was worth about $15,000, because Pete only signed them for about a month before Nick left the room. There were twenty albums signed only by Mike, Dave and Willy the Wanker, and they were real collector's items because of the limited number and association with a historic occasion. Steve confiscated them at the time, and he was able to laugh about it later when he saw what they went for.

Halfway through the tour the fans stormed the stage. There was a lot of confusion. Nick, Mike and Dave made it to the car and they assumed Pete was in another car. So they got back to the hotel and there was no sign of Pete. All night there was no sign of Pete. In the morning there was still no sign of Pete.

What had happened was that Pete had managed to hide in the van of one of the roadies. After a while the van took off. When it stopped Pete got out. He started walking and after a while he reached a street with some stores. There was a drugstore, and a liquor store, and a store called Five and Dime—all very American. Every once in a while someone would look at him, and twice someone screamed PETE!!!!!!!! and asked for an autograph.

He kept walking down the street, looking at the stores and the people and the American cars. He had the feeling that the world was very quiet, that he was hidden in a part of the world that was just quietly going on while Steve imploded.

He had a hundred-dollar bill in his boot, which was the only item of clothing that could not easily get ripped off by a fan. He went into the Five and Dime and bought a check shirt and a pair of straight-legged jeans. He put on the new clothes and threw away the old ones, and now not so many people looked at him. Then he went into a barbershop that looked like the kind of place his father went, and he asked for the kind of haircut his father always asked for, and when he went back out into the street no one looked at him.

He walked out of town and put out his thumb, and he was picked up by a man in a white Chevy pick-up truck. There was still that quietness in the world.

The road stretched straight out ahead looking just the way he always thought an American road would look. The radio was on. The driver appeared not to be one of his fans.

Well I know I'll be blue
If my true love's untrue
I don't think I could ever bear to part
Don't you walk out the door tomorrow
Leaving me to grief and sorrow
Cause I'll beg or steal or borrow back your heart

The world was so quiet. Eat your heart out, Paul McCartney.

And that was the end of the Breaks. Pete kept going east on Route 66. People would stop and he would open his mouth and they'd say You're *English, aren't* you? and nothing was too good for him. Sometimes they'd drive through a town past a record store and he'd see pristine copies of Groovin On Down in the window and they'd just keep going. After a while he went south and it was just as American though different and he saw places where you'd see tarantulas hopping down the road and people would actually say Howdy and he never got tired of hearing it. In one place he bought a harmonica, an instrument that is a lot harder than you might think. He spent a lot of time going MWA mwa MWA mwa getting the hang of it. He would never be anonymous again.

•

In 1998 *Bike Magazine* had a special Harley Davidson issue with an insert including a piece on the Harley Owners Group (HOG). It really is a way of life, said a member, with any other motorcycle you pay up at the shop, buy the bike and that's it, but with a Harley that's just the start. He said it was all to do with meeting likeminded people who knew that you didn't need to do 160 mph everywhere to get a buzz. He said you ended up with friends all over Europe, the tours meant that you met people with the same biking interests as you, but with varied backgrounds.

I said

The berimbau is a unique percussive instrument, consisting of a gourd with a single string. Played with a bow, it produces tone with a beat! Much used in Brazil, the berimbau will add that unmistakable 'samba' sound to your music, and will make you the envy of all your friends.

We are sending you this remarkable instrument in the hope that you will sponsor Anya, daughter of a former musician. Anya, a hardworking student, is keen to go to college. Sadly, Anya's father Nick is unable to help Anya achieve her goals. That's why we need people like you. People who remember all the pleasure musicians like Nick have given in the past. People who want to give the younger generation a chance.

We hope you'll help Anya, Pete. But whether or not you choose to help this deserving young student, the berimbau is yours to keep.

Pete said What the fuck?

I put the berimbau and the bow on his keyboard.

I said I want to be a banker. I want to make six figures. I don't want to sell shit on a market stall.

Pete said And Nick won't give you the dosh? The mean bastard.

I said I'll pay you back. It's three years and a year in Egypt.

I explained the connection between Arabic and six figures. I said I needed four figures a year.

Pete said Is that all? He dug under a lot of papers and he took out a chequebook and he wrote a cheque for five figures.

He said Hey! hey! hey! Anya! Don't cry! hey! hey!

He said Let's see how this little fucker works.

He took the bow and bounced it softly on the string and he sang

O I can't do the boogie woogie
I can do the oogie doogie
O won't you oogie doogie with me?
Oogie woogie doogie
Oogie woogie doogie
Oogie doogie baby with me

He looked up and he said You know Nick

He said

Nick, you know, he was into that rock thing, people watching, the money

He said

You know, just before our US tour we were in Gibraltar and I went over to Africa 'cause I didn't think it would take that long to get back. It was just after our second album came out, and Steve had changed a lot of shit to make it like the first album. And that album was really popular, the fans didn't notice, so I felt like the fans were total wankers. I felt betrayed. And Steve had booked us for a whole year of gigs, just playing the same shit the same way every time.

So I walked along the beach, and I didn't know what to do. I thought it would be better just to walk into the water and die than go through the year, and I couldn't understand how they could do it. They turned my life into something worse than nothing, into this torture, for the sake of extra sales, well couldn't we just have had enough sales and something in it for me? And how could they just decide like that that my life didn't matter, it didn't matter if I was in, like, agony. But the thing is they didn't know they were doing it. They didn't know what they were taking away because they never had anything real to know what it was like when everything was a fake. They could get a lot of money and blag about the business. The money was the only thing there could be for them, and they'd never have anything else.

He said

Don't get so you can't have anything but money, Anya. You don't want to be like Steve.

He said

But what the fuck, do what you want.

He said

Booga dooga dooga

De white man sucks

Booga dooga dooga

He really sucks

He said

I like this baby. Hey!

Trevor

'It is really a very sobering thought,' said Trevor, 'and one which the local talent, I'm afraid hasn't quite cottoned on to, that a painting of a beautiful subject is almost invariably a rotten picture. Guaranteed kitsch, in fact, don't you think?'

Lily and Trevor were sauntering along the Cherwell in the University Parks; it was late afternoon in early July, and the drowsy calm of the sky, the languid sway of the trees, the deep shadows cutting sharply across the grass, all so fondly, so lamentably repeated on a dozen or so canvases, did seem to bear him out. The faintest, merest, tenderest hint of a blush in the sky reminded, with beautiful delicacy, that evening was coming on; several paintings gestured at this moment, but even the least little touch of pink gave them an air of digging an elbow in the side of the spectator, of announcing 'the approach of even' in a carrying stage whisper.

'It just goes to show that a little pink really does go an *awfully* long way,' said Trevor.

'And how,' said Lily. She spent most of her conversations with Trevor agreeing with Trevor, so much so in fact that the conversations were at times positively Socratic—at least in the variety of ways Lily found to express assent. But as they stood looking back across the park (they had reached the duck pond) she was struck by the unity of tone of the pale hot sky, the pale trees moving on the hot air: the wonderful tranquillity of the scene seemed to owe something to its evocation of sketches in chalk or pastel. And those stands of trees in open ground or clustered by the river—those lovely masses of foliage—for Lily, at least (but then she was American), part of their charm lay in being so very much the sort of thing she had admired in the Constables in the Ashmolean. That did not, of course, mean that the principle was wrong. There were all those wrecked ships by moonlight, naked girls with dabs of impasto at the nipple, all those sunsets over the desert to sustain it.

But then, she pursued doggedly, what about Botticelli? Did one not suppose him—had he not supposed himself—to have been painting beautiful paintings of beautiful subjects? Venus? Primavera? Was it perhaps simply a sign of our time that it was impossible to be Botticelli—that now painting the beautiful remained firmly within the province of Maxfield Parrish? So that the relation of painting to beauty was perhaps something that must be referred ultimately to socioeconomic factors: and all because Botticelli was not kitsch. Or *perhaps*—and here she nearly stopped in her tracks at the audacity, the sophistication which she fathomed, suddenly, in Trevor's aperçu—perhaps an argument could be made, taking a larger view, that by certain lights Botticelli *was* kitsch.

And it was only at this point that her speculations, at first a mere trickle which might as well flow subterraneously as not, swelled to a stream which must come to the surface sooner or later, ought indeed to have been out in the open all along.

'Was Botticelli kitsch, would you say?' she ventured. Who can say what Meno or Polus was thinking underground, to give themselves such an appearance of being incapable of proper argument?

'Oh,' Trevor exclaimed now, 'if everyone were a *Botticelli* ...' a little impatiently, for his own stream of remarks had been gurgling and chattering in the sunlight briskly on, and had just been coursing down a little cascade of cheery murmurs about tea, so that the abrupt cessation of the agreeable warm undercurrent of consent, the eruption of an earlier current of conversation in a geyser at the foot of the fall, were chilly, unwelcome surprises. They had turned up the avenue which runs parallel to Norham Gardens (Trevor lived at the top of a mustard-coloured house overlooking the park), and after a brief pause (the waters eddied furiously around the intrusion),

'What shall it be?' Trevor resumed genially. 'Shall we go back to my place? Or shall we try a tea shoppe?'

Lily weighed disagreeables: Trevor's square tea of St Michael's Tea Assortment, the longer walk to the nearest tea room.

'The Wykeham's a bit of a walk, but it's a nice day.'

'We'll go back to my place, then, shall we?'

The easy habit of Trevor's stride, as he turned down the fork which led out to Norham Gardens by Lady Margaret Hall, reproved the false answer as clearly as his words. Lily was in general more acute, but was distracted by the impression that she was rising, for the first time, to the level at which Trevor's conversation was pitched. The prospect of scones and sandwiches and cake might have leavened her earnestness; intellectual endeavour seemed only right, however, now that a note of austerity had been sounded, and discussion was to march forward on rations of crumbling chocolate digestives, vanilla sandwich cremes, pink wafers and ginger nuts. 'We *know* that he is not—but how do we justify it?'

Alas that the Socratic method should be at times so mal à propos! Trevor was patting his pockets for his keys, he glanced up with a charming rueful smile as they reached the street. 'Oh, you Americans! Are you ever *not* philosophical?'

'Oh, but *you* started me off! *You* launched us into aesthetics!' cried Lily playfully, for the descent to personalities was too marked a change of subject to be missed, and flirtation seemed the only apology for her earlier obtuseness.

'I strike a generality once an hour, I believe. And then, like a good British worker, I break for tea.'

•

The tin of St Michael's Tea Assortment lay open on a low table. A ginger nut and two sandwich cremes reposed, undisturbed, on a plate on Lily's lap; a plate by Trevor's side held half a plain digestive, crumbs from whose other half drifted down his delightful tie. Two cups, half-drunk, of Earl Grey flanked the biscuit tin. Half a pot of Earl Grey sat stewing within a red knitted tea cosy.

The scene was, to Lily, a little dreary. Her gaze moved about the familiar room — the dark brown wall-to-wall carpet, the Morris armchairs upholstered in a repeating pattern of a hunting scene in pale brown on off-white, the huge squashy red-and-brown striped sofa on which they were sitting. Snatches of colours, of textures, of patterns she had come across came to mind, like felicitous phrases, fragments of Cicero or Tacitus to the mind of a Latinist glancing through a poor composition. On the walls were a couple of daguerreotypes of Trevor's great-grandparents (appropriated not without some acrimony from other members of the family); two black-and-white enlargements of photographs of Cretan peasants; a small oil of a young gentleman with his horse, c. 1772, clothes, expression, posture, horse all carelessly comme il faut — a several greats grand-uncle of Trevor (more spoils from family property); and a Dutch genre painting of a woman mending. Lily considered these in relation to the question of kitsch. Trevor leant back into the corner of the sofa, crossed his legs, finished off his digestive.

'What was that you were saying about Botticelli?' he asked now benignly, brushing crumbs off his fingers. The modest comforts of the squashy sofa, the St Michael's biscuits, the Cretan peasants had, it seemed, fortified him for argument.

Lily felt, for her part, somewhat chilled by the largely glum décor. 'I thought that might work as an example of paintings of beautiful subjects which succeed in being genuinely beautiful themselves.'

'But it's precisely the success, isn't it, that sets them apart? That's not much of a conundrum.'

'Well ...' She thought that she could, after all, have spoken more fluently over, say, a plate of scones with clotted cream and strawberry jam. 'Does that mean, then, that any unsuccessful painting of a beautiful subject must be kitsch? Isn't there more to it than that? Aren't there all kinds of mediocre paintings of beautiful things that aren't, I don't know, in bad taste?'

'I suppose it's the note of sincerity, a sort of shamelessly yearning, passionate sincerity, that's so damning. It's embarrassing to watch, isn't it—like seeing someone in a state of ecstasy with his fly open.'

'Perhaps that's it.'

'So what I was getting at earlier,' he grinned, 'was that a state of ecstasy leaves one terribly prone to forget to "adjust one's clothing".'

Lily smiled.

'Can I tempt you to another cup of tea? I'll make fresh.'

'Yes, *please*,' she said brightly, and began eating one of the sandwich cremes in the interests of conviviality. The red knitted tea cosy was borne off to the kitchen.

'I think that's rather sweet, don't you?' He returned to find her standing in front of the young man and his horse. 'Early Gainsborough has even been suggested. I don't totally buy that, but it's nice that the thought is in the air.'

'Is that based on style, or is there some Gainsborough it might be?'

'Oh, I don't know the ins and outs of it. There are far too many, unfortunately, that it couldn't possibly be—all the really good ones, I'm afraid. But Gainsborough or no, it has a certain charm. Or does family pride make me partial?'

'Oh no, it's *delightful*!' she cried, for if politeness required assent, a note must be struck of firm conviction if assent was not to sound merely polite.

'I came by it by rather devious means, which some might say don't do me much credit—but my trophy more than makes up for the occasional pang of conscience. The pangs, in any case, are far more occasional than is entirely decent. It's a rather amusing story, though it may shock you—or have you heard it before?'

This was a question which admitted of only one reply, which she promptly gave, as plausibly as a person could who had heard the story twice before.

'It belonged to my great aunt Sophy,' Trevor explained, as he returned to his seat and began to pour out. 'She lived in the same house for fifty years, a big old Victorian monster crammed to the attics with everything she'd picked up over the years—most of it junk. She never threw anything away, and never let anyone else in the family do so either, it was a kind of family joke—if anyone said they were thinking of getting rid of something, it was always the very thing she was looking for. She'd no children of her own, so it was always assumed that her treasures, such as they were, would go to her brothers' and sisters' children. Eventually, no doubt, things would trickle down to the great nieces and nephews, but my chances of getting anything worth having were pretty thin. The odds were that I'd get a box of chipped crockery or a pair of mildewy opera glasses. No one imagined for a moment that she'd bother to make individual bequests, so there were understandings about suitable recipients for some of the more interesting items. There was an understanding—a pretty vague one—that Great Great Great Uncle Harry here would go to my cousin Harry, who'd said he fancied it because of the name. I'd seen it on a couple of visits to Great Aunt Sophy, and wanted it, but couldn't see much chance of getting it.'

'So how *did* you get it?'

'Sheer opportunism! I happened to be staying with some friends down in Sussex one year, and ended by seeing quite a lot of Sophy. (Don't smile!) I suggested to her that it would be a terrible shame if everything were to be auctioned off indiscriminately. Of course it was highly unlikely, but it worried her. She asked my advice; I suggested that everyone be asked to pick out the items of particular interest to them. She insisted I take my pick on the spot! I allowed myself to be persuaded, and ended by taking home with me the Gainsborough query portrait of Harry. My cousin Harry will hardly speak to me, which is a kind of added bonus—he is probably the most boring man in the country.'

She had by now, of course, a certain amount of practice in replying to this story, but still found it hard to know how one should react to an anecdote which showed Trevor in so disagreeable a light. Why did he tell the story? Why did he tell it to her?

'Have you ever thought of having your own portrait done?' she took a running leap at what looked the nearest patch of solid ground in the marsh. 'Or do you have a portrait of yourself?'

'Only what you have given me.'

What was he talking about?

'Come and see.'

The adjoining room was fitted up as a small study (Trevor was an editor at the University Press, but also kept up with 'his own work'). Six-foot-high bookcases surrounded the walls, except for a space left clear for the desk; above the desk, in a Perspex frame, is an enlargement of a photograph of Trevor taken by Lily several months earlier. Lily has a copy of it herself, it is one of the best things she has done. The grain of the black and white, the gaze directed in contemplation quite inaccessible to the camera; the three-quarters profile, permitting the face the interest of the unobserved, neither closing itself off from nor grinning manically at the camera, but reflective, full of its secrets—all these have worked so happily together that the particular features of Trevor—the very flat, broad forehead, the long straight eyebrows, pale grey eyes, the long, thin, mobile mouth, seemed in the very nervous texture of their individuality to be the occasion of harmonious tranquillity.

'You should have asked me for the negative,' said Lily. She has given Trevor a print, since it is always nice to have a good picture of oneself; she had not realised how much Trevor would like it.

'It's very soothing to my vanity to have this. Mine's really a very boring face—or else the mirror has been lying for years.'

'Oh, I don't know. They say the camera never lies. Of course, there are always passport photos—it makes you wonder if all cameras *can* be telling the truth.'

'I sometimes wonder whether the mirror doesn't tell us only how we see ourselves. Cameras may be truthful about the way others see us—I shouldn't expect passport photographers to have a particularly agreeable perception of humanity.'

'Probably not.' But did she have an agreeable perception of Trevor? Did the photograph not suggest, in any case, that to be interesting was all that mattered? Was hers an interested eye?

'Have I ever told you about my youthful passion for photography? I was a sort of infant prodigy with a Brownie—even won prizes in national competitions, though in the amateur category, of course. I've got the scrapbooks somewhere or other—must show you them some time, if you wouldn't find it too boring.'

'I'd love to see them.'

'I'll see if I can find them. Can I get you a drink?'

'Yes, *please*.'

Lily stood in a corner of the sitting room. She held a glass of dry sherry (she preferred cream). In a mirror above the mantelpiece she saw, mute tones further muted, the backs of the two armchairs, one row of biscuits in a tin, the edge of a teapot in a red tea cosy, a red-and-brown striped squashy sofa in three quarters profile. Reflected, framed, the room had charms foreign to the original, just as an ordinary or even ugly object gains beauty and dignity when painted or photographed. Trevor came in with a fat scrapbook and sat down on the sofa.

'The reflection gives the room great charm, don't you think?' said Trevor. 'But it depends a great deal on where you stand. Move a little this way, that will give you the best angle of vision.'

She moved a few steps towards the door. Trevor's knee, an arm resting on the knee appeared with the frame.

'No, just a bit further over.'

A few more steps, and Trevor came fully into view.

OXFORD, 1985

Plantinga

You reach a stage where they ask you for a biography or a CV. Sometimes it's for a catalogue. Sometimes it's for a grant application. And of course, if you're a photographer, this is alien to your practice. It doesn't matter whether you use a darkroom or digital manipulation; the image always develops over time, in ways beyond your control. So what does it mean to put a label on this or that event?

Plantinga was born in Berlin in 1956 to an Estonian mother and unknown father, thought to have been a journalist.

You can say that she was given her first camera at the age of 17. That she was working as an au pair in Amsterdam. That it was a Leica; that it was the prized possession of Maarten, dead brother of Matthias, father of the family. It seems as though you should say, she was bitterly disappointed, because she wanted a Polaroid: it's definitely the case that our timebound relation to technology has been a preoccupation. She has 100 cameras and lenses beyond count. The name Plantinga marks the acquisition of the mechanical eye.

This is the case: when she uses the Leica, she always wonders what dead Maarten would have made of what she sees.

She had read Stanisław Lem's *Bajki robotów* in German, *Robotermärchen*. Robot tales. She could not find it in Dutch. She told the stories to the children, playing robot games. This would turn out to be important.

This is the case: if she had done a degree she could put down the degree.

She took a job as au pair with a family in Oxford. The husband was a barrister, the wife a solicitor. They told her for £30 she could go to lectures at the university. Her English would not have been good enough to do a degree. If she had been doing a degree she would have been tied to a syllabus. When the children were at school she went to lectures on philosophy, on Linear B, on the Umayyads.

There was a Czech dissident, Julius Tomin, who lectured on Plato. He had given illegal seminars on Aristotle in Prague, where he had had to dodge the secret police; a group of Oxford philosophers had rescued him. At first the lectures were crowded, he filled a big hall. Later he was ostracized. He was stubborn in the way that dissidents have to be. He could not teach to the syllabus. He had a controversial theory that the *Phaedrus* was Plato's first dialogue. He would give a class in the Philosophy Sub-Faculty and maybe two people would come. The rest of the time he would do something no professional academic could do, he would sit all day every day in the Bodleian. There are signs saying no photography is allowed, but the staff are not always in every room; she could get pictures of this wrongheaded Platonist at work. She could go to all these lectures on philosophy because she was an au pair, and he could give them but nobody would come because they were not useful for the syllabus.

Was the Phaedrus *Plato's First Dialogue?* : 1982–88

Of course she took pretty pictures of the pretty town. She sold them for postcards.

She read Calvino's *Invisible Cities*. She read Goffman's *Interaction Ritual*. She read Crozier's *Le phénomène bureaucratique*. It was in the Philosophy Sub-Faculty that she found A. C. Danto's *The Transfiguration of the Commonplace*. She took pictures of graduating students; she talked about Linear B, the Umayyads, interaction rituals. She would say: How is it possible for physically indistinguishable objects to be different works of art? The students had lively, engaged, yet poignant expressions: destined for Arthur Andersen, for merchant banks, they discovered too late their lost chance to learn Linear B. Of course these were popular photographs. Of course it was easy to get more commissions. Of course it was easy to be asked to weddings and bar mitzvahs. It was not so easy, of course, to know what dead Maarten would have made of it.

The Woodfords taught her to play bridge. This would turn out to be important.

An economist taught her to play poker. This would turn out to be important.

This could go on and on but it can't go on.

Cultiver son jardin : 1988–2002

In 1988 Plantinga rented a room in East Dulwich from the Estonian minimalist Liis Rüütel. Rüütel had squatted a house in Bermondsey with the installation artist Andrew Hopkins; had learnt construction techniques (plumbing, wiring, plastering, carpentry); had taught at Goldsmith's and Central Saint Martins; had bought a condemned house for peanuts, restored it, rented out rooms, and given up teaching. She would say that her painting got all this energy from the fact that she was not teaching, she was not putting all this energy into the students. Because Plantinga was not a student, because she was just living in the house, she was there at this burst of energy. The attention was directed entirely at the art and not at her, so that's paradoxical, that she would get more than she would get from the thing you put on a CV. She could go to the studio and hear the words that happened to come, words hitting the air the way paint strikes a canvas, not congealed to the illusion of authority, of definitiveness, that you get from a text on a printed page. She could see something you don't see so much in a gallery, the historical development of the artist, the work the artist has left behind next to the new. And then there was this other thing, there was the transmission of the praxis of Andrew Hopkins into the plumbing and a kitchen cabinet and a light fixture and after a while a conservatory at the back, you would have these dense minimalist paintings next to the fixture, these different flows of things going through the hands. It goes without saying that you can take pictures. Of course after a while they want you to take pictures for catalogues.

It doesn't go without saying. When she was a child she blocked out Estonian. If her mother spoke to her aunt she would disunderstand, because her mother spoke comical German and it was embarrassing. But Liis Rüütel had this mastery of English, she could articulate a point about the Kantian sublime and explain how to disconnect the water supply to a sink and then effortlessly use words like *wally* and *boffin* and *bollix*, if she wrote an advert on eBay to sell a toaster you were completely transfixed. So it was as if Estonian had been developing for 30 years in the brain of Plantinga, if Liis got on the phone to her sister comprehension would click into place, Liis would get off the phone and Estonian words would come suddenly to the mouth that would not speak to its aunt or its mother, and at the same time it was as if the brain had been waiting for concrete proof that English was possible for an interloper, it clicked into place—if you are a photographer you notice when something teaches you about time.

And then there was a different period. Rüütel's gallerist took 20 paintings to Frieze and it was a sensation, they all sold within hours, so of course Liis thought it would not be necessary to rent rooms. But the gallery kept not sending money, there were these long conversations on the phone, and each time Liis would go into the garden and dig and plant and put down paving stones. Plantinga wasn't living there any more but each time she went back there would be this new transformation of the garden or maybe a new upstairs kitchen. So of course these are pictures that have to be taken before you know what to do with them, you come back and there is a pond with a natural waterfall and a rocky basin and carp and a Japanese maple. It's like, if you go to the Colorado River you see where the water has cut down through the layers of rock through the millennia.

She played poker at the Vic on Edgware Road.

She played bridge at the Young Chelsea Club. She really did.

You have to remember that she had gone to seminars on the *Philosophical Investigations*. She could develop her thought on language games and interaction rituals. She could pay the rent and buy kit without schmoozing her gallerist. She had posh friends who played Flannery Two Diamonds & thought nothing of buying 5 prints.

Getting Ready for Dinner with a Gay Friend : 2003–4
The Role of Expressiveness in Human-Robot Interaction : 2003–4

This was a bit mischievous. Well, it was bad. It was bad. Ivo is not on speaking terms with her, so yes, it was mischievous.

She got a place as artist-in-residence at the Robotics Institute at Carnegie Mellon in Pittsburgh. There is a big Polish population in Pittsburgh, so what she did was, she got people to make recordings of *Bajki robotów* in Polish, and then she got a guy at the institute to make robots that would tell the stories, and then she made a video of autistic children interacting contentedly with the robots.

So Pittsburgh, as maybe you know, is built at the confluence of three rivers; you can take a trolley car up to the bluff overlooking the city and you get a view of the rivers and these dozens of little suspension bridges which you have to love. She ran into a girl who said someone had offered to pay her rent for a year. He wanted to take a photograph of this view as seen from the interior of an apartment in which someone was living in a completely natural way. All she had to do was move in and furnish it the way she would naturally. His idea was that she would be engaged in some kind of activity, ironing napkins or something like that. What he wanted was to juxtapose this ordinary, everyday activity with the traces of this steel town.

Ordinary! Everyday! She could see that the girl was completely gobsmacked.

The girl was an art student. She did not even have an iron. She did not even have paper napkins, if she had people over for a meal she would tear off paper towels. But as soon as she moved in she bought an iron and an ironing board, and she bought some cloth napkins, and if you are going to have cloth napkins maybe you need a tablecloth so she bought a matching tablecloth. And maybe she would have reverted to natural behavior, but Ivo kept saying, I just want you engaging in some ordinary, everyday activity, something like vacuuming, or dusting. So of course then she had to buy a vacuum cleaner and a dust cloth, and of course Ivo would come over to experiment with the light at different times of day so she would feel the apartment had to look presentable for the kind of person who thinks vacuuming is an everyday activity. So she became fanatical about housekeeping, she would vacuum, she would wash all the dishes and put them away, she bought a teapot and a creamer and a sugar bowl and a little tray and a glass plate for cookies.

It was like an extreme form of this phenomenon that's really common, which is that when you have gay friends to dinner you suddenly remember that they had hand towels and scented soap in the bathroom and you are conscious of living in squalor. Or at least, she thought it was like this phenomenon, but that was just the perception of the possessor of the mechanical eye. She had some money at this point. She rented an apartment, and she found a girl to live in it, and she said she would leave her assistant to handle the details. One of the reasons she loved gay bars, of course, is that there is this fanatical attention to detail, and they cosset you, so you become aware that you can ritualize looking after someone and that doesn't devalue it. So she asked Ed Vittorini, who ran her favorite bar, if he would take care of this; she said she was going to want the inhabitant engaged in some ordinary, everyday activity, and he should just get her to act naturally, live naturally in the apartment. And of course, as it turned out, the end result was these two girls in an apartment with an ironing board and cloth napkins and a matching tablecloth and a tea tray and something in a clothes bag that had just been picked up from the dry cleaners and a vase of fresh flowers.

Entourage

He went to Krakow for no particular reason.

He had found a flight for 5 euros; for an additional 9 euros one could take a suitcase weighing 20 kg, or 44 pounds. He packed a small suitcase with books.

He went into a bookstore and began opening books. A sample of randomly encountered words:

wzsyedł

gwiezdnie

wszystko

zwyciężyć

Note the frequency of the letters z, w and y. The sample is, in fact, unrepresentative; in a larger sample of Polish words the letters j and k are also common. Couple of sentences:

Żył raz pewien wielki konstruktor-wynalazca, który nie ustając, wymyślał urządzenia niezwykłe i najdziwniejsze stwarzał aparaty.

Żył raz pewien inżynier Kosmogonik, który rozjaśniał gwiazdy, żeby pokonać ciemność.

•

He had once read a collection of *Robotermärchen*, robot tales, in German. A translation of some stories by Stanisław Lem. One had naturally not grasped that the word "gwiazdy," whatever it might mean, featured in the original. One had not understood that the title of the original was *Bajki Robotów.*

It was now unexpectedly necessary to purchase a small suitcase and fill it with books replete with the letters z, w, y, j and k. It was necessary to hire someone to fly with him to Berlin to accompany the suitcase. Słowosław was the applicant whose name had the best letters.

His life was quite difficult at this time for reasons we need not discuss. It was often necessary to travel. One never knows how long one will be gone, you see. If it's just an overnight trip one might manage with a couple of old favorites, but once, you see, he went to Bilbao and was unexpectedly kept hanging about for weeks.

He took the precaution for a while of booking a second ticket and hiring someone to bring a second suitcase. It's not just that it was beginning to be complicated to bring an extra bag; it's so much easier, obviously, if the bag is accompanied by someone able to carry it for you.

To all intents and purposes that should have been perfectly adequate for unexpected contingencies, but the fact is, one had to mull over the candidates for the second suitcase. He still needed the whole of the indispensable collection which had filled the first suitcase, but now he had *Bajki Robotów* to consider, not to mention others too numerous to mention.

He would travel, at any rate, to, as it might be, Istanbul with his first suitcase under his own supervision and the second suitcase in the care of an escort, and on arrival in Istanbul would discover all sorts of books that one simply never sees. Books, you know, with a dotless i. Umlauts up the gazoo. It would be necessary, obviously, to purchase a new suitcase and hire someone locally to fly back with it.

An American need never learn a language to communicate. One should choose a language the way one chooses a dog or a musical instrument.

He went to Copenhagen at one point. The Danish word for island is Ø. The common run of visitors do not see the phenomenon as necessitating purchase of a suitcase and hiring of a Dane.

He had seen ø described as a monophthongal closed mid+front rounded vowel. Reliable sources informed him that this was the sound of the vowel in British "bird" or, in the light form, the vowel of French "bleu." His approach was to sit in a café in Copenhagen and lure one of the natives into recording *Odins Ø* in GarageBand on his MacBook. On a subsequent occasion he sat in a café in Oslo and lured an unsuspecting native into selecting a book from the suitcase and recording a passage.

It's interesting, everyone knows that Perec's *La disparition* is a book in which the letter e does not appear, but *Rabbit, Run* is never mentioned as a companion piece in which the letter å does not appear. Ångstrom being the correct spelling of the surname of the eponymous protagonist.

It's better to bow to the inevitable. It's really simpler, you know, to purchase the empty suitcase and hire its minder before one sets out. In Catalan the letter x proliferates. The word for fiction is ficció. He was unable, in the event, to find a Catalan at short notice in Berlin; an ad on the Barcelona Craigslist turned up Francesc.

Those were the early days. The days when he could make do with one additional packed suitcase plus carrier and one empty suitcase, ditto.

He noticed at some point that one could fly EasyJet to Bilbao, 10 people, each with 20 kg of checked luggage, for £346.90. A mere £34.69 per person.

In the later days if he had to go to Bilbao he would book one ticket for himself and 20 for the entourage.

It would have been simpler in many ways to put the entourage up at a hostel in 12-bunk rooms but he could not bring himself to do it. He had tried it once but it had been a mistake. It had been necessary to replace the gossipy backbiting entourage with a clean new entourage.

He would be getting on with things, minding his own business, be dragged into conversation, leave, leave a message for a member of the entourage to join him in Ürümqi.

The books are marked with colorcoded flags. They have marginal notes.

He buys books to remind himself to read them.

At one point it looked as though he might have to replace a member of the entourage. Francesc was having a fit of the sulks. It was by no means clear that a Xavier or Xulio would not be a better man for the job.

He found that the best way to go about it was to be very casual, post on Craigslist.

With an entourage of 20, there was always the possibility that someone would have to be replaced.

Each member of the entourage was a native speaker of the language in which books in the accompanied suitcase were written. When he wanted to know how a passage should be pronounced, when he wanted to get the sound of the words in his head, he could have a recording made in GarageBand on the spot. One can't find this kind of thing on the Internet. So one could not have a single pinch hitter, one needed the full complement of languages accounted for in the second string. At some point he realized that he needed to hire someone to manage the entourage, to keep understudies ready.

Ideally one would have an understudy waiting in each city. There is never any telling when a member of the entourage will simply up stakes.

It wasn't the sort of thing he should be doing for himself. He tried to hand it over to his lawyer. His lawyer handed it over to someone young and stupid who made careless mistakes, the work was not important enough to merit competence.

"Look," he said. "It's perfectly straightforward. One simply wants a carrier to match the suitcase. When you buy a suitcase you don't walk in off the street and pick the first thing you see, you select it for aesthetic properties superfluous to the task of transporting possessions. The name of the carrier is an aesthetic property. The language spoken by the carrier, on the other hand, must match that of the books contained in the suitcase for strictly utilitarian reasons, as he or she may be required at any time to record material from one of the books in question. It's necessary, therefore, to recruit, in each case, a substitute who both speaks the language and bears an appropriate name."

The young, stupid lawyer said he was not sure he would recognize an appropriate name.

He pointed out that a simple expedient would be to recruit replacements bearing names identical to those of the current incumbents, a solution one might have expected a graduate of Harvard Law School to work out independently.

An inconclusive exchange of compliments ensued.

His lawyer charged $450 an hour, $200 for the services of the halfwit. Money that would mean a lot to the sort of person who worked in the entourage. The sort of person who worked in the entourage might in fact be the best sort of person to recruit for the entourage.

It was necessary to return to New York for reasons we need not discuss. He put an ad on Craigslist and conducted interviews at Circa Tabac, where it was permitted to smoke.

Between interviews he talked to Siobhan behind the bar, explaining the ins and outs of the entourage. For a putative tip of $10–$25 an Irish bartender will offer quiet sympathy, not to say Gaelic charm, in a way that not only a hot shot $450-per-horam lawyer but also the hot shot's $200-per-horam entry-level wannabes will emphatically not throw in with the billable hour.

A woman at the bar said her husband had won a sushi restaurant in a poker game. It had been closed down for violations of fish-related hygiene issues; the proprietor had shortsightedly complied with the letter of the law, neglecting the spirit of law enforcement. She had commented. Her husband had walked out, leaving her with two small children to raise.

"You wouldn't happen to be looking for a sushi restaurant," she said. "They tell me the sushi train alone is worth fifteen grand."

A girl at the bar, a fiery redhead, told him he should be ashamed of himself. He should do something for his fellow man.

He was about to protest when he saw suddenly that something could be done with the sushi bar. As a child he had loved *Charlie and the Chocolate Factory*.

The mother-of-two had left. He darted to the door, scanned the street to left and right, descried the wretch in the middle distance, dashed in breathless pursuit.

Twenty children could be placed round the perimeter of the conveyor belt! Color-coded tasks could be assigned! The child would have the chance to amass points! Points would entitle the child to select a plate with a cake, cookie, chocolate, or other delight from the moving belt!

Skipping up and down, he wears a bow tie.

Studies have shown that a talent for delaying gratification is integral to success in our complex society. In the abovementioned studies the child is presented with a marshmallow, told it may eat at once; if it waits it may have a second marshmallow. It's absurd. What sort of incentive is a marshmallow?

What one wants, surely, is to encourage industry by tapping into the longing for immediate rewards. One wants to offer the child the opportunity to win one chocolate after another. One wants, perhaps, to determine which sorts of chocolate are most efficacious.

One might install a sushi belt in every school, allowing access to only the hardest working students.

Prancing bow-tied on the pavement he explains his vision.

Money being no particular object he was soon in possession of the fabled sushi belt, with accompanying restaurant.

The peerless Siobhan found him an entourage manager, in whose capable hands he left the task of recruiting 20 children.

He had more money than he knew what to do with.

Presently he had more children than he knew what to do with.

Competition for a place was soon fierce.

Being perforce an autodidact he had read Barbara Godwin's *Justice by Lottery* and been entranced. It is inarguable that, in a hereditary monarchy, the position of head of state is distributed, in effect, by lottery, the lottery of birth, and that the occupant is then trained for the position, and arguable that such a system might work better for any number of occupations than the present system in which, at every stage, purely educational aims are often subsidiary to the requirement to signal ability. The lottery need not, of course, be the lottery of birth. There is likewise no need, of course, for its allocation to be final; a five-year stint, if memory serves, was the recommendation of Godwin, though one could no doubt make a case for others.

With only 20 places to work with he did not want to wade through a flood of applications (he was sure to be flooded with applications once word of the excellence of the system got around). How much simpler simply to give a place to the first 20 children with attractive names. (Being an autodidact he had read extensively on the subject of fast and frugal heuristics as outlined by Gerd Gigerenzer of the Max Planck Institute.)

The names of the first 20 hopefuls were not as interesting as the names of his entourage. Many applicants had names like Matthew and Josh. The names of the first 10 members of the entourage, just to give an idea, were Þorvarður, Øyvin, Øllegård, Jäärda, Håkan, Ferenc, Franzyska, Knut, Xulio, Txomin. (He had agreed with the manager that the names of the entourage should remain fixed, though temperamental bearers might come and go; it was simple enough to advertise for the desired denominations.) He managed to come up with Niamdh, Cesangari, Amartya, Zygmunt, and Dzsó before retreating to a least worst selection. (A spirit of mischief, honesty compels us to confess, led him to arrange a separate session peopled entirely by bearers of the name of Josh.)

He had all sorts of ingenious schemes. Schemes for mastering the Cyrillic alphabet. (He had been entranced to discover that the Russian for Protopope was Протопоп.) Schemes for mastering logarithms, trigonometric identities, simple differentiation. There were all sorts of exercises; upon correct completion, the child might select a cake from the traveling belt.

Each session lasted three hours. Children had to be sent out to play.

He had delusions of grandeur. A sushi train presumably costs less than incarceration. Might the device serve as a preventive to juvenile delinquency?

He saw presently that one might place small tables, each seating 8, perpendicular to the belt. With a little judicious tinkering it was then possible to seat 160! Each table was supervised, you see, by a member of the entourage. It was really very light work.

A love of pet projects ≠ talent for dealing with government ministers.

When a child misbehaved it was expelled never to return.

When asked he stated that he was studying the role of chocolate in academic performance.

Was chocolate more efficacious than ice cream? Might some children respond better to one, others to the other?

He had once read a book by Orlando Patterson, *Slavery and Social Death*. Being of necessity something of an autodidact he had taken the book to heart. Patterson claimed that in the days of the Romans slaves often preferred the latifundia, plantations where slaves performed backbreaking labor but lived otherwise without surveillance, to the easier life of the household slave. Who cannot understand this? And who cannot understand that a child might be happier, in many ways, earning its keep than living the life of a pampered pet?

The children earned points for spelling čokoláda and cioccolata.

The Josh session could not have come at a better time.

If one is going to do the thing properly, one wants Borges read by an Argentinian, Vargas Llosa by a Peruvian, García Márquez by a Colombian. And so on. Sometimes, though, one doesn't want to clutter up the mind. It was simpler, he realized, to settle on a single, easily memorable name for the Hispanophone contingent. He chose Julio. Within a short time he had Julio Argentino, Julio Chileno, Julio Boliviano, Julio Peruano, Julio Venezolano, Julio Colombiano, Julio Salvadoreño, Julio Mexicano (and so, of course, on) at his disposal. Similarly, one wants an Egyptian, of course, to read Mahfuz and el-Ghitani, a Syrian for Adonis, and so naturally on, but an entrepreneur needs to prioritize, it was simplest, he found, to recruit a cohort of Hassans. Who could then be distinguished as Hassan al-syriani, Hassan al-libnani, Hassan al-maghribi, and what have you.

Every once in a while a squabble would blow up among the Julios or the Hassans, but he now had an entourage manager (thank heavens!) to pour oil on troubled waters.

He devised ever more ingenious challenges, coupling them with ever more elaborate incentives.

Let us suppose a menu of possible tasks and rewards. A possible task is the performance of problems in algebra presented in Hungarian. The reward is a 5-tier wedding cake. (As an incentive, it beats a pootling little marshmallow into a cocked hat.)

He saw presently that it would be a mistake to try to establish a chain of schools. One is subject to so much unwelcome supervision. What was wanted, surely, was a chain of child-oriented *restaurants*. The sort of place where a parent could leave a child at any time day or night. Everyone cannot afford the fees for a private school. One might be able to afford a session or two a week at an educational restaurant. One might be able to send a child full-time to the restaurant while flush, then fall back on the public school system when funds ran short.

He threw himself headlong into development of the chain, which he envisaged as a crossbreed, uniting the best features of Dunkin' Donuts, Baskin-Robbins and YO! Sushi. Within 2 years he had franchises in New York, Washington, Miami, Boston, Providence, Philadelphia, Chicago, Kansas City, San Francisco, Los Angeles, Denver, Seattle, Portland, Minneapolis/St. Paul. The Josh-only sessions proved surprisingly popular. (It was, as it turned out, possible to fill a 160-seater with Joshes.)

•

Rich people don't care what happens to you.

One day he discovered, by a happy accident, that he could streamline the entourage.

He had happened to purchase a DVD of *Harry Potter and the Philosopher's Stone* in Barcelona. One could watch the film, it emerged, dubbed into French, German, Dutch, Flemish, Danish, Italian, Brazilian and "Portugal" Portuguese, Spanish, Catalan, Basque, Greek, Hungarian, Turkish, Czech, Slovak, Polish, Norwegian, Swedish, Finnish, Bulgarian, Romanian! Welsh, Irish, and Scottish Gaelic! Croatian! Mandarin! Japanese, Hindi, Tamil, Punjabi, Urdu.

He sat curled up on the sofa in his hotel suite.

It's much simpler, obviously, if each suitcase does not have to be supervised by a native speaker of the language contained in its books: one can then have, as it might be, three suitcases per person. One can manage quite nicely, for instance, with a complement of Julios and Hassans.

He put a Josh in charge of the restaurant chain. The boy had won 1,597 individually wrapped Reese's Peanut Butter Cups, 326 chocolate oranges, 861 Eskimo Pies, 119 pints of Ben & Jerry's Chunky Monkey, 200 5-lb bars of Hershey's Chocolate, and 21 5-tier wedding cakes. One would hardly look to find a better qualified candidate through more conventional means of recruitment.

Publisher's note

Readers will notice that American and British usage vary in *Some Trick*. Stories set in the UK follow British usage; stories set in the USA mostly follow American. However, when America is viewed through British eyes (for example, in "My Heart Belongs to Bertie"), British usage will be found.

In "Famous Last Words," some readers might find that the use of X and x causes some confusion. The author's unpublished novella *Paper Pool* makes all clear:

I never show my story to Simon. I show my story to Nick [not his real name], who says:

'Is this about you? Who's X, one of your boyfriends?'

'Of course not,' I say. 'It's a variable.'

'It's a natural thing to think.'

'It is *not* a natural thing to think,' I say. 'The whole point is that it could be anybody. It works like a pronoun, only it gives less information, we don't even know if the character's M or F.'

'Of course he's a guy,' says Nick. 'It says so.'

'It does *not* say so,' I say. 'It says X.'

'But he's *obviously* a guy. All that talk about politics.'

'Exactly,' I say. 'So we see how far the reader goes beyond what's actually there, you know how much is constructed, so that specifying *corporeal* properties seems to tell us something we already know.' It occurs to me that this is a trick with all the conceptual sophistication and avant-gardist chic of *The Mysterious Affair at Styles*.

'I still maintain he's a guy,' says Nick. 'And how come he changes from a capital X to a small x at the end? You have to admit that's *deliberately* obscure.'

'It's *not* obscure, it's a totally different variable,' I say. 'You might as well say it was confusing to have a character named David and another one called Dave. And you see we never do know what little x is. The dark blue trousers are just trousers—what a great line. And so true.'

'Hmmm,' says Nick.

(And the equation featured in "Famous Last Words" has been drawn from *Mathematical Analysis: A Special Course*, by G. Ye. Shilov, translated by J. D. David, and edited by D.A.R. Wallace (Pergamon Press, Oxford).)

Rachel's SUDO MAKE ME A SANDWICH t-shirt in "Climbers" quotes *xkcd* #149, "Sandwich," with permission of Randall Munroe. Readers who would like to own this excellent t-shirt can find it at https://store.xkcd.com/collections/apparel/products/sudo.

Author's note

In the Renaissance blue was an expensive pigment; a patron commissioning a painting would specify how much blue the painter was to use. Fiction today has its own prohibitively expensive pigments. Edward Tufte took out a second mortgage on his house to self-publish his spectacularly handsome first book; this meant he could marshal a crack production team. The writer who lacks his resources has a couple of options: 1, try to persuade skeptical agents to find a publisher who will provide technical support; 2, spend hundreds of hours coding, hundreds more grappling with Adobe Illustrator, and so on. "Long and winding road" and "Faint but pursuing" are my two most common e-mail subject lines. "Dear Paul, THANK you for your help with ArabTeX!" is typical content.

Over the years visitors to my blog (paperpools.blogspot.de) have generously helped me live to fight another day. While *The Last Samurai* was out of print buyers of secondhand copies would send donations to the beleaguered author. More recently two dedicated readers have been thinking of ways to approach the challenge in a less haphazard manner; anyone who would like to be involved should contact me at helen.dewitt@gmx.net to be put in touch. Readers who would like to sustain an author wandering the labyrinth of Stack Overflow can buy me a coffee at https://ko-fi.com/dewitt.